We hear this is the testing Site →

★

TESTING REGION

THE FROZEN SHORES

Beware...
Crevasse open
and close regularly

TUNDRA

WITHDRAWN

THE FROZEN SEA

Fastest Route to the Testing Site

RELIC

THE BOOKS OF EVA

HEATHER TERRELL

RELIC

THE BOOKS OF EVA

SOHO
TEEN

Published in the United States by Soho Teen
an imprint of
Soho Press, Inc.
853 Broadway
New York, NY 10003

Library of Congress Cataloging-in-Publication Data
Terrell, Heather.
Relic / by Heather Terrell.
p cm—(The books of Eva ; [1])
HC ISBN 978-1-61695-196-2 (alk. paper)
International PB ISBN 978-1-61695-439-0
eISBN 978-1-61695-197-9
[1. Fantasy.] I. Title.
PZ7.T274Re 2013
[Fic]—dc23 2013008769

Interior illustrations © Ricardo Cortés
Interior design by Janine Agro, Soho Press, Inc.

Printed in the United States of America

10 9 8 7 6 5 4 3 2 1

To Jim, Jack, and Ben

History of New North

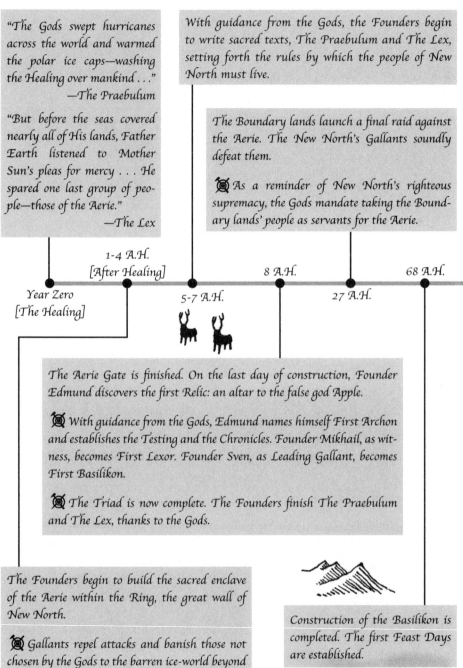

"The Gods swept hurricanes across the world and warmed the polar ice caps—washing the Healing over mankind . . ."
—The Praebulum

"But before the seas covered nearly all of His lands, Father Earth listened to Mother Sun's pleas for mercy . . . He spared one last group of people—those of the Aerie."
—The Lex

With guidance from the Gods, the Founders begin to write sacred texts, The Praebulum and The Lex, setting forth the rules by which the people of New North must live.

The Boundary lands launch a final raid against the Aerie. The New North's Gallants soundly defeat them.

As a reminder of New North's righteous supremacy, the Gods mandate taking the Boundary lands' people as servants for the Aerie.

1-4 A.H.
[After Healing]

8 A.H.

68 A.H.

Year Zero
[The Healing]

5-7 A.H.

27 A.H.

The Aerie Gate is finished. On the last day of construction, Founder Edmund discovers the first Relic: an altar to the false god Apple.

With guidance from the Gods, Edmund names himself First Archon and establishes the Testing and the Chronicles. Founder Mikhail, as witness, becomes First Lexor. Founder Sven, as Leading Gallant, becomes First Basilikon.

The Triad is now complete. The Founders finish The Praebulum and The Lex, thanks to the Gods.

The Founders begin to build the sacred enclave of the Aerie within the Ring, the great wall of New North.

Gallants repel attacks and banish those not chosen by the Gods to the barren ice-world beyond the Ring: the Boundary lands.

Construction of the Basilikon is completed. The first Feast Days are established.

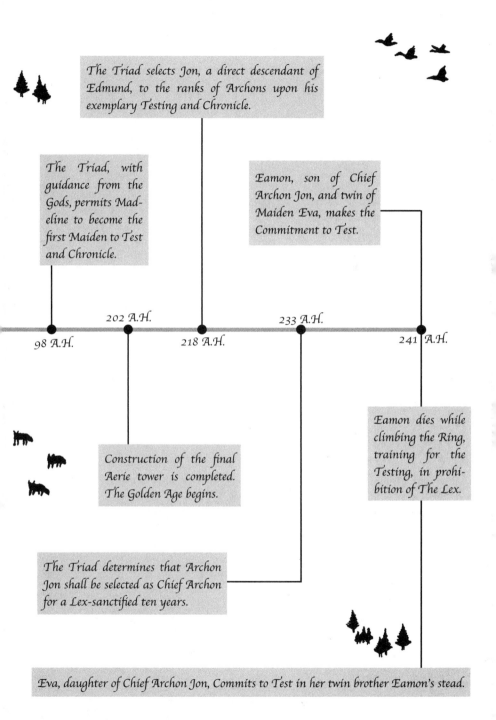

The Triad selects Jon, a direct descendant of Edmund, to the ranks of Archons upon his exemplary Testing and Chronicle.

The Triad, with guidance from the Gods, permits Madeline to become the first Maiden to Test and Chronicle.

Eamon, son of Chief Archon Jon, and twin of Maiden Eva, makes the Commitment to Test.

202 A.H.

233 A.H.

98 A.H.

218 A.H.

241 A.H.

Eamon dies while climbing the Ring, training for the Testing, in prohibition of The Lex.

Construction of the final Aerie tower is completed. The Golden Age begins.

The Triad determines that Archon Jon shall be selected as Chief Archon for a Lex-sanctified ten years.

Eva, daughter of Chief Archon Jon, Commits to Test in her twin brother Eamon's stead.

Prologue

Eamon throws his axe into the ice above his head. He hits a perfect depression in the wall. Pulling up hard, he kicks the bear-claw toes of his climbing boots into the wall. He repeats the practiced motion, over and over. Like some kind of arctic cat, he scales the frozen Ring.

Each time he moves, he makes sure to insert an ice screw level with his waist and secure his rope to it. Just a precaution should he fall. Not that he ever has.

Bit by painstaking bit, the top of the Ring nears. Although he knows he shouldn't, that it goes against the primary rule of ice climbing, Eamon can't resist: he looks down at the hundreds of feet of sheer ice below.

Even in the dim moonlight, the vista makes him dizzy. The Ring, a near-perfect, mountainous circle of ice, stands at the center of this last remaining land above the seas, his home: New North. It makes the risk of climbing—punishable by exile into the Boundary lands—worthwhile. That, and the edge it will give him for the Testing.

He looks back up. Despite the cramps in his hands and calves, he smiles a little. Only a few feet left to the summit. Just one more swing of his axe, and he'll be standing on the peak.

He drives his axe hard into a hollow. But he is too hasty. For the first time ever, he misreads the ice. The axe doesn't hold. It slips out of the giant, slick wall.

Sliding backward, he plummets twelve feet. He bounces off sharp outcroppings that lacerate his skin. His descent is stopped only by a screw, his rope, and his harness. Dangling upside down in the frigid midnight air, hundreds of feet from the ground, he starts to pull himself up.

As he manages to right himself, he sees that his rope is frayed.

How, Eamon can't imagine. He had made the rope himself with sealskin. He was certain of its strength. But the reason doesn't matter. All that matters is how he'll climb the remaining twenty feet with an injured body and a worthless rope.

He begins to unhook himself from his harness, and the slight pressure makes the rope unravel farther. Just before it snaps and yanks him down with it, he swings his axe into the ice. Shaking and bleeding, he clings to the face of the ice wall with only his axe and his bear-claw boots. He has no choice but to climb back up, this time creeping inch by inch.

Stupid. He should never have risked the Ring, no matter the possible advantage. He needs to win the Archon spot, to make sure he can act on what he's learned, but he didn't need to try the Ring. Pride and thirst for glory brought him to this place. He'd assumed the Testing would be the easy part, given his training and sure footing. The difficult part was to make sure that his Testing Chronicle secured him not only the Archon Laurels, but also the Chief Archon spot when his father's term ends. But he forgot the rule drilled into him from infancy: don't presume to know the ice and snow. Now he stands to die. *That price* is not worth what it will do to Eva; he won't be around any longer to protect her. The only consolation is that, even if he lives, sharing the truth with New North might get him killed anyway.

He sees the summit. As he plans how he'll hoist his damaged body over the lip, a silhouette of a figure appears against the backdrop of the moon. Instinct tells him to scale back down. The Ring-Guards and certain exile await him at the top. But he knows his only chance of survival is surrender.

"Over here," he calls out.

The figure moves toward him, leans toward the edge, and stretches out a hand.

Eamon leaves his axe in the ice so he can reach. "Thank the Gods, you're here."

A hand clasps Eamon's, and the figure's face becomes clear.

"What are *you* doing out here?" Eamon asks, too confused to be frightened.

"I'm so sorry, Eamon. You were never meant to make it this far."

The figure lets go. And Eamon falls from the Ring into the darkness.

I

Martius 31
Year 242, A.H.

I stand on the turret, watching the night fall. The Ring looms large in the darkening horizon, and I can't avoid looking at it any longer. Not if I want to say a proper goodbye to my dead brother before I set off for the Testing. I gaze at its steep, jagged ice-cliffs, but it's not enough. I need to get a closer look—as eye-level as possible—and stare straight at the place that killed my brother.

Eamon, my twin. I can barely even think his name. I'm not ready yet, but I have no choice.

Lifting up my heavy fur cloak and my long Feast-day skirts, I step up onto the ledge of the turret. I've been up here hundreds of times before with Eamon—the turret was our special place—but it takes me a tick to get my footing.

My delicate ceremonial shoes don't have the same grip as my *kamiks*.

I steady myself, and try to relax. My breath forms an icy cloud in the encroaching polar darkness, and I start to shiver. Not just from the cold. Fear of getting caught out here has got me shaking. The punishment for disobeying The Lex by being here after the None Bell—especially tonight, on the Feast of the Testing—is severe.

But here I stand. I must.

The Moon is generous with Her light, and I can see clearly. The glistening Aerie spreads out before me, like a diamond encircled by the mountainous icy Ring. The Aerie fortress of ice and stone is the place where all the Founding Families live and work and learn and worship. It is home.

I stare out at the frozen land. Just over the turret's edge, I see the ice walls of the School with its fancifully carved ice windows gleaming in the low moonlight. I spot the imposing ice-spires of the Basilika, the place for worship and instruction on The Lex. Only a glimpse of the Ark in the far distance coaxes a brief, sad smile. The only metal and glass structure in New North, the Ark is our most precious place, where most of the island's food is grown. Within its warm, humid walls, I had hoped to find my calling.

No more. The innocent Maiden who longed for a peaceful life in the Ark is gone. She died on the Ring with Eamon, and she became someone else. Sometimes I don't recognize the determined girl who replaced her, the one who insists on pursuing her dead brother's dreams of Testing. And neither do my poor parents. It's a cruel trick to play on my father, who is meant to be celebrating his final year as Chief Archon. He's not meant to be mourning his son and lamenting his daughter's choices.

I take a deep breath and force myself to take another glimpse at the Ring. I can make out the place from which Eamon fell. It looks oddly beautiful in the pale blue moonlight, not murderous. I stretch out my hands toward it. Then I close my eyes for a brief tick, hoping to imprint the image on my mind forever. As if I could take Eamon with me in the Testing tomorrow.

"Eva! Get down from there!"

Lukas. I don't need to turn to recognize the voice. Before Eamon's death, we three were close friends, despite the fact that Lukas served as Eamon's Boundary Companion. Since Eamon's death, I've spent most of the past few months training for the Testing with Lukas. But it isn't Lukas's words that scare me; it's his tone. I hear fear, and he is always calm.

"Eva, get down now! That snow is *quiasuqaq*. One more step and you'll fall."

I cannot move. Lukas knows snow better than anyone. If it is truly *quiasuqaq*, then even the smallest false move will send me sliding off the ledge and flying hundreds of feet down. Just like Eamon.

"Stay still," he orders.

I hear his footsteps running across the turret. His hand clamps down on my arm and pulls me down toward him. We fall backward on top of each other, both of us breathing heavily. I struggle out of his bear-like grip and turn around.

I look into his dark, almond-shaped eyes. "I just wanted—"

"I know what you wanted, Eva. To be close to Eamon."

He alone understands what Eamon's death has done to me. And I think I know what Eamon's death has done to Lukas. Even though we never speak of it. Even though I pretend for everyone else.

"Yes," I answer.

"You know, Eva, you don't have to scale turret walls or Test to be close to him. Eamon will always be with you. His spirit is *anirniq*. Or *animus,* as you Aerie say."

His words cut through me. I swallow, my eyes stinging. I won't sob. I've spent the past few months trying so hard to be strong, trying to push down the desperate sadness I feel at Eamon's death, trying to prove I can fulfill his Testing dream for him. Lukas's words nearly bring me to the brink. I can't have that. So I stand up, brush the snow off my gown, and grasp onto the least sad thing I can think of.

"Let me guess, my mother sent you up here to fetch me for the Feast. I can almost hear her." I raise my voice in a loud whisper, an affectation my mother assumes to sound like the ideal Lex Lady. "'How dare Eva break The Lex tonight? After all she's done to embarrass this family! And in her father's last Feast of the Testing as Chief Archon!'"

Lukas chuckles a little, indulging me. "No, she didn't order me up here. I volunteered for the job."

"No one else was up for the task of the turret at night?"

"Fair enough." His laughter fades, but his smile holds. "We should go down. They're all waiting for you to begin the Feast of the Testing. Maiden of the bell."

I smile back at him. It feels good to have him teasing me again. Since Eamon's death, he's been so formal, as if he could avoid the truth by respecting the frozen barriers that are supposed to exist between us.

He offers me his arm. I gather the long folds of my cloak and gown and take a firm hold of his elbow. I look up at him. Despite his dark hair and eyes; flat, high-cheekboned face; and vast height and breadth—none of which fit the

Aerie model for handsomeness—he's somehow attractive. Not that I'd ever think of him that way.

He places his other hand over mine. Together, down the precipitous, winding stairs, we descend.

II

Martius 31
Year 242, A.H.

The moment we enter the solar great room, Lukas drops my arm. He disappears into the busy hive of dark-haired, dark-eyed Boundary Attendants lining the wall or scurrying in and out of the kitchen. I must face the room by myself.

The hearth-fire is almost too much for me to bear after the icy night air. My family and friends stand before it, warming their hands close to its orange-red flames. In the flickering light of the dozens of lamps and candles, I can see they are all wearing their Feast finery—dark gowns and tunics, heavily embroidered as The Lex requires, somber against the vibrant flames.

For a brief, blissful tick, no one realizes that I've returned. I feel an urge to flee back out into the pure, white cold. Back to my solitude. Back to Eamon. But then my mother looks up from the blaze. I freeze in my tracks, feeling icier than I'd felt up on the turret. I know that expression. She may appear the perfect Lady with her gentle smile and elegantly outstretched hand, but I know anger seethes beneath— anger that will manifest in ever more restrictions for me.

Somehow, I must repress the girl from the turret. For the benefit of my parents and our guests, I must become, once again, the Lex-abiding Maiden I used to be. I think on the admonitions for Maidens: *be ever pleasing to the eye and ear.* I paint a smile on my face and demurely lower my gaze.

"Eva, my darling. An Attendant has been out searching for you. Our friends are here with blessings for tomorrow. But there was no Eva to bless!" My mother adds a laugh as she picks at the embroidered sleeve of her gown. I know that I should've been here, waiting for Jasper and his family to arrive, as well as respecting my own relatives. What excuse would a Maiden offer? I stammer a bit, trying to think of the perfect answer. One befitting my station. One acceptable to my mother.

Jasper comes to my rescue. Ever the Gallant. Faultless in his brown tunic, trousers, and fur mantle, he rushes to my side with an easy laugh. With his fair Nordic looks, it's hard for me to imagine that one day our parents' shared dream of a Union might actually come true. He seems too perfect. Although, of course, the decision about a Union belongs to our parents and the Triad.

"Were you hiding on the turret, Eva? You naughty Maiden! I can't believe you forced poor Lukas out onto those slick stairs on a frigid night."

Jasper says it in jest, not realizing the truth of his words. The tension breaks, and our guests break into smiles and chuckles. Jasper always knows the right thing to say, especially in front of my mother. I'm thankful for it, but worried Lukas has heard Jasper talking about him that way. I scan the row of Attendants for sign of him, but then I catch my mother standing with her mouth agape. She realizes that I *was* actually on the turret, even though The Lex mandates that Maidens must be indoors after the None Bell for their protection. I brace myself for her reaction.

"The turret?" My mother's voice slips into Lady-pitch, as if her high whisper with its perfect adherence to The Lex somehow makes up for my recent lapses. I wish she'd relax her standards and leave me alone for just one night, or at least not publicly hint at her complaints. It's humiliating. But no matter how furious she is with me for my errors, she's careful not to accuse me; she has worked too hard to mar the image of our Lex-perfect family now. Even Eamon's death hasn't shaken her resolve.

To my great surprise, my father answers for me. "Eva will be Testing in the days to come, Margret. I don't think we should worry about The Lex tonight."

"But Jon . . ." Her voice has that Lady-pitch again.

My father is insistent. "No more, Margret. Tonight is the Feast of the Testing. I am Chief Archon. And we have a Testor in our family."

My mother quiets; she has no choice. The Lex clearly states that a wife follows her husband's commands. That goes triply for the wife of a Triad Chief.

My father gestures to an Attendant along the wall to bring forth a tray of goblets. It's my own Boundary Companion, Katja. Once each guest and family member has received the mead from Katja's tray, my father raises his own goblet.

I look around at the circle of extended family, mine and Jasper's, all with their cups lifted high.

To the left is my mother's family—her sister, husband, and two children, and her brother and his wife—so distinctive with their white-blonde Nordic hair and pale blue eyes. In my mother's mind, their pure Nordic blood almost makes up for the fact that her brother and sister aren't Lord and Lady, but mere Gentleman and Gentlewoman. Neither is a Keeper or married to one; neither was as shrewd as my mother, or lucky enough; her brother is just a Steward to another Keep and her sister married a Steward as well. To the right stands my dad's family—his brother, his brother's wife, and their young son—so like my dad with the inky hair, pale skin, and narrow eyes of the Russian people. Still, my mother affords them the respect they deserve, as my father's brother is a Keeper. Only the Triad of New North leaders—the Lexors, Archons, and Basilikons—rank higher than Keepers. And the Three Chiefs rank highest of them all during their terms of service.

With our auburn hair and green-blue eyes, Eamon and I used to tease each other that we belonged to another family, maybe even random Boundary parents. My mother couldn't tolerate jokes that we might come from any stock other than pure Founding; after insisting that we were a throwback to a rarer bloodline, she'd banish us to our bedrooms for nasty talk.

Scattered throughout the group are Jasper's family: his parents, his sister, and an uncle with his wife. They are a more mixed group than mine with a strong North American streak, but still pure Founding stock all, and not only Keepers in their mix but a Chief Lexor too, Jasper's uncle Ian, and his wife. Even though the circle consists of eighteen people, it seems small and incomplete with-out Eamon. Especially since Jasper was always Eamon's friend, not mine.

I hold my breath. I can't imagine what my father will say.

"In the morning, the Testing begins. Our children, Eva and Jasper, will be among the Testors. The competition will demand much, more than we have already sacrificed." My father pauses uncharacteristically—he's usually so comfortable and smooth in his speeches—and the room is absolutely still. Everyone understands exactly what he means by that sacrifice.

His voice takes on a commanding Chief Archon tone, the one I've heard so many times in the Aerie town square. Suddenly, he sounds like he's giving a speech to New North instead of initiating the Feast of the Testing. It seems out-of-place at first, but then I realize that he might break down over Eamon if he doesn't act the Chief Archon instead of a father. This Feast was always meant for Eamon. Not me. And the Feast was meant to secure the Gods' blessings that Eamon return not only with the Archon Laurels, but also with a Chronicle worthy of the Chief Archon position when my father's term ends later this year.

My father incants the ritual language. I've heard this every year of my life, but never in the context of my own participa-tion. The words are as familiar to me as my own name. "The Lex says that, on the night of the Feast of the Testing, we shall tell our children that we Test because of what the Gods did for us when we survived the Healing. Over two hundred years ago, the Healing washed over the Earth, leaving only the Gods' chosen people alive. The Gods—our mother, the Sun, and our father, the Earth—delivered us to New North, the Gods' chosen land. The Gods gave us a final chance to redeem mankind's evil by living in accordance with their Word—as written down in The Praebulum and The Lex.

"The Gods told our Founders that we needed a Triad of strong leaders, ones who could teach the New North people the dangers of our past, like worshipping the false god Apple. Leaders who could show the people we must live in accordance with The Lex, which dictates mankind live as we did in the Golden Age of the Medieval era, that idyllic time before the false neon of modern advancements set mankind on a path to wickedness and lawlessness. Thus, the Gods formed the competitions for the sacred roles of Lexors, Basilikons, and Archons—among them the Testing for Archons."

I raise my eyes and lift my hands—cup and all—toward the heavens, as my father asks the Four Sacred Questions for the Feast of the Testing.

"Why is this night different from all other nights?" he intones.

"Because, on this night, we ask the Gods to bless our Testors as they prepare for their sacred trials." I hear myself give the ritual response, along with the rest of our guests, though my mind is with Eamon

"Why will tomorrow morning be different than all other mornings?" my father asks.

"Because, in the morning, we will ask the Gods to bless our Testors as they make the Passage and set off on their hallowed journey," we answer in unison.

"Why will the next twenty-seven days be different than all other days?"

"Because, for each of those twenty-seven days, we will join together in the town square for the Gathering—to offer prayers for the Testors' safety and for news of their Gods-given triumphs," we say together.

"And why will the twenty-eighth day be different from all other days?"

"Because, on the twenty-eighth day, the Gods will choose our new Archon, a leader capable of surviving the journey to the Frozen Shores, discovering Relics that washed onto the Frozen Shores during the Healing, and writing Chronicles about the Relics that will show the New North people the rightness of our Lex-sanctified ways."

We raise our cups. Normally, we drink together as the final step in the ritual. But tonight, it seems that my father has more to say. I wonder if he will address the end of his term as Chief. The Lex does not require it, but many Chiefs throughout the ages have made farewell speeches. If not tonight, surely he will do so another evening, though I might not be there.

"Tonight, we lift our cups to the Gods that either Jasper or Eva is chosen as the Chief Archon from this Testing. Certainly, they are both worthy of New North's highest calling. But whether or not the Gods judge them deserving, we pray that they return home safely to the Aerie. *Benigno numine.*"

As I raise my goblet to my father's, my hand shakes in relief and gratitude. My father's words sound like a begrudging approval of my insistence that I Test. I don't want him to mistake my trembling for fear. I've worked too hard these past months to secure approval for him to think I have even a moment's hesitation.

No one was more astonished than my parents when I announced my Commitment to the Testing. Eamon was heir designate; he alone had the years of physical, scientific, and historical training to withstand its rigors. In the wake of his tragic death, both my father and mother insisted that the Testing was not the place for their pretty, slender, and demure Maiden. My father had hoped I would choose a life better suited to my talents and gender—perhaps as a Master Gardener in the Ark, at least until I became the Betrothed of Jasper, our mothers' greatest wish. Though either of those pacts had yet to be formalized.

But try as he might, my father couldn't find anything in The Lex to stop me from Testing, even when he appealed to Chief Lexor, who also happened to be Jasper's uncle and a close friend. Besides, I'd practically memorized The Prae-bulum and Lex in an effort to convince him. No amount of emotional pleading deterred me from submitting my name. Not even the persuasive, ever-logical arguments of Jasper swayed me. In the end, my father stopped resisting. He even let me train with Lukas as Eamon had, always with a proper Lady chaperone of course. My mother seethed, but this wasn't about her. This was also something that my father knew intuitively. Because it wasn't about me, either. It was only and always about Eamon.

My twin's life ended on the Ring, but his dream did not. And I would never allow that dream to die.

By the time my goblet touches my father's, my hand is still. He nods at me. The serving horn sounds, and he, as Chief Archon, motions for our guests to follow my mother into the Feast. One by one, we dip our hands into the cool, clean water of the proffered silver wash basin.

As a Testor, I go last, right after Jasper. As my fingertips graze the water's surface, I try to keep my eyes cast down. But I can't. I know Lukas is holding the silver basin. I want to thank him for saving me on the turret—thank him for all he's taught me, really—but he stands at the wall, gazing blankly in the distance like the perfect servant. As if we are both invisible.

I position myself to meet his gaze and stare straight into his eyes for a long, long moment, so he has no choice but to acknowledge me. At once, I wish that I hadn't. In that darkness, I see something that moves me more than any pleading by my parents over fear for my safety during the Testing, or any carefully plotted arguments of Jasper. I see sadness.

III

Martius 31
Year 242, A.H.

The last bell before Evensong sounds. Never have I been so happy to hear the tolling of the *Campana* that dictates every tick of our existence. The bell means that our guests must leave, taking their endless chatter about the glories of past Testings along with them. I can't stand another tick.

Painful. That's what the past two bells have been, not that I've revealed my discomfort. With a gracious Maidenly smile on my face, I have endured bells of stories from relatives and friends. Last year, I listened in wonder. These are the stories that form the core of the New North. The true legends about how age-old winners braved the indomitable ice to make unprecedented discoveries. The true legends like the one that made my father Chief Archon.

"Remember the gown they found years back?" Jasper's uncle Ian cried after a few too many meads. As Chief Lexor, Ian rarely smiles, let alone laughs, but tonight is a special night. The lines in his face, etched as harshly as the stones on the floor, wriggle with secret delight. "The one without the sleeves?"

The Ladies and Gentlewomen tittered appropriately at the notion of a dress without sleeves. Modesty is at the very heart of The Lex: *other than that of your face and hands, let no swath of skin be seen by the Aerie or Boundary men of New North.* Females are in need of the Gods' special protection. Besides, what of the exposure to the elements?

"Or the gown that rose above the knee?" Ian's wife bandied back. With this, the Ladies and Gentlewomen gasped. This sort of debauchery was almost too much for them to imagine, even with their bellies full of mead. My father raised his voice, "That will be enough of the scandalous talk." But he exchanged a knowing smirk with Ian.

Of course this, too, was part of the ritual: these long-winded exchanges of artifacts the Testors uncovered—not just the immodest clothes, but dangerous remedies, Apple amulets, and even one rare Apple altar, the empty glass surface where the pre-Healing people spent countless bells staring at themselves in false worship—each meant to be more shocking than the last. I also understood they were meant to embolden me and Jasper for the days ahead. But they didn't. All the talk about artifacts just reminded me of my major Testing weakness.

Lukas taught me the ways of arctic living so that I could stand a chance in the early Test Advantages where the Testors prove their survival skills. Still, I don't know enough about the world before the Healing. Testors typically dedicate years to learning about pre-Healing history so they can identify artifacts and craft cautionary tales, an act that is the very heart of the Testing and the Triad's efforts to reinforce the critical message of The Praebulum and Lex. Instead, I spent my School days studying the Ark and perfecting the ways of the Maiden, neither of which will help me in the Testing. All my time training with Lukas can't make up for this flaw.

At the final warning gong before the Evensong bell, my muscles ache from keeping still. The desperation is a fever: to race up to my room away from all the chattering guests, muster my courage in private, and count down the bells until dawn. But I assume my Maiden duties. As befitting the daughter of the Chief Archon, I rise from my chair and stroll to the front door for the formal farewells. They seek my father's blessing and *vale* first. Then, taking each guest's hand in my own as The Lex for Hosts require, I thank them for their blessings.

My manners falter only when I reach Jasper, the last in line. Tomorrow we'll be fellow Testors. So strange that we've known each other our whole lives; he was friends with Eamon, after all. And his uncle and my father are so very close.

But there's something else. Something that I only consider now. Recently I've felt his eyes on me. I've seen him flustered, as if he feels something other than simple friendship or the bind of family ties. As if he might feel the same way as our families about a Union. Not that I've been in a frame of mind to really consider anything other than my grief and the Testing. Regardless of how either of us feels, I know that everything changes as of tonight. How we speak to one another, how we look at each other, even how we think about the other. We'll become fierce competitors. Not friends. Certainly not more than friends.

The expectant gaze of my parents and his parents bears down on us. This, too, is a test. I take Jasper's hands in mine, and look into his face. I see my unspoken words reflected in his eyes. I say all I can under the circumstances, the ritual blessing for those few permitted to journey beyond the Ring. "May the Gods travel with you."

"May the Gods travel with you also."

With a last squeeze of my hand, Jasper ties his fur cloak around his waist and disappears with his parents out into the frigid night.

Lukas closes the heavy stone door behind our guests and bolts it tightly. I see a slight softening in the rigid block of his shoulders, and even my parents breathe an audible sigh of relief. The ritual is over. We can relax.

The solar great room begins to darken as the servants extinguish the candles and lamps. Just as I start toward the stone staircase, I hear a heavy tapping at the door.

We all freeze. No one knocks on doors in the ticks before Evensong Bell when all inhabitants of the Aerie must be in their homes. Only the Triad—the Lexors, Archons, and Basilikons—have the right to move freely at any time. Lukas's body stiffens, and he glances over at my father, who nods permission for him to unbolt the lock. We stand at the ready.

I see the distinctive fur mantle before he steps into the room. It's Jasper. He and Lukas exchange glances but not welcomes—Lukas is only a Boundary Companion, no matter how highly regarded.

Jasper bows deeply to my father. "I'm so sorry, but I had to come back," he offers, his face a mask of contrition for my parents. "I accidentally left my great-grandfather's sealskin cloak behind."

"The cloak Magnus wore while Testing?" my mother asks, her voice whispery again in its Lady-pitch.

I know he's lying. There's no way he'd forget that cloak. Before the guests had lost themselves in drink, much of the dinner conversation was devoted to Magnus's exploits, who won his year's Testing to become the Archon. According to the legend, Magnus had made it to the Testing Site in record time. And Jasper's mother made a very public display this evening of giving Jasper the cloak for luck in his own Testing.

"The very one," he says.

"Oh, well, you must have the cloak for tomorrow!" my mother exclaims, "Eva, help Jasper find it. Quickly."

I follow Jasper into the dining hall, trying to figure out what kind of game my mother is playing, though I can guess. She wants Jasper to have luck. She wants him to win, and for me to lose but return alive, so we can be Betrothed, and the awful tragedy of Eamon's death can be forgotten in the wake of a new beginning. As we peer under the heavy trestle table and search under the benches, I get a much closer look at Jasper's sandy hair and light blue-green eyes than The Lex normally allows. He looks more real, more vulnerable than his public Gallant appearance.

"I had to come back, Eva," he suddenly whispers. "To say a real *vale*."

I blink back shock. Jasper always abides by The Lex; he has faith in its importance to the survival of the Aerie people. That he might break a cardinal rule like observance of the Evensong bell, just to say goodbye—it's unthinkable. Not to mention he just lied about his reason for being here, something else The Lex strictly forbids: *let no untruths pass over your lips or through your hearts.* Then again, my mom knows. She must.

Jasper smiles at my astonished expression. Despite the circumstances, I can't help but smile back; his grin reveals the lighter side under that constant dutifulness. He usually keeps it hidden under lock and key. I know that, rather than smiling back, I should protest. In fact, the proper Maiden reaction would be to admonish him for taking the risk and for his audacity. He's speaking out of turn for a Gallant, after all. Professions related to Unions can never occur without parents as witnesses—and, only then, once formal agreements have been entered at the parents' initiation and the Triad's approval. But I want to hear what he has to say. So I stay quiet.

"I've spent a lot of time over the past few months trying to get you to not Test," he says.

"I lost count of your legal arguments at a hundred. You might consider serving as a Lexor if the Testing doesn't work out." I'm nervous at what Jasper might say, and my sorry attempt at a joke just slips out. A Maiden should be more solemn: *let no humor cross your lips unless invited by the Gallant, Gentleman, or Lord in your company.*

Jasper smirks, but he quickly recovers. "I'm sorry I couldn't give you the support you needed, Eva. It must've been really hard for you to listen to me when you were already dealing with so much over Eamon."

"Your protests didn't help." I don't see any sense in denying it, no matter the niceties demanded by normal Aerie conversation. Given that we're already in flagrant defiance of The Lex right now, honesty seems the only course.

"I need you to understand now why I tried to talk you out of Testing."

I nod. The Lex forbids the Testors to speak to one another for the duration of the Testing. More than one Testor has been sent back to the Aerie for violating that single rule. "Okay," I say quietly.

Jasper breaks our gaze and stares down at the rough floor before continuing. "Eva, for a long time now, I've hoped that we could have a future together."

I can't help but wonder if my mother anticipated he'd make this confession as a last ditch effort to make me withdraw. My heart pounds. She'd be taking a huge risk, but of course, she could deny everything. Unions are strictly the purview of parents and Triad. Not Maidens and Gallants. A part of me is flattered; Jasper is considered one of the most eligible Gallants in the Aerie. But still, I don't know how I feel about him. I haven't allowed myself to experience any emotion since Eamon died. I'm fearful that, if I let in a single sentiment, the floodgates of grief will burst. Then I might as well withdraw.

I don't want to commit to anything right now, and I definitely don't want to insult him. Nor do I want to give my mother a victory. So I say as little as possible, using her logic. "I understand. It wouldn't be appropriate for a future wife to Commit to the Testing. No female has competed for over one hundred years."

Jasper looks up from the floor and grabs my hands. "That isn't it at all, Eva. You have as much a right to compete as any other Founding family member. You proved to us all there are no Lex rules stopping you. And I don't care what your mother or my mother or anyone else thinks about your behavior and The Lex for Maidens . . ." He pauses, blushing. "It's just that I can't stand the idea of you getting hurt, and the Testing is dangerous. I couldn't go on if something happened to you."

I open my mouth, but no words come. I have no option but to hide behind my Maiden mask of modesty. Lowering my gaze, I manage, "Oh."

"Eva, I'll do whatever I can to help you during the Testing, no matter The Lex, no matter—"

"Jasper?" My father's voice bellows from the solar. "Have you found what you are looking for? Evensong will ring momentarily."

I glance over at Jasper. He pulls the sealskin cloak out from under his fur mantle, where it had been all along.

"Yes, sir. I think I have."

IV

Martius 31
Year 242, A.H.

The floor and bed of my bedroom are strewn with preparations. Bags containing maps and books; *kamiks*, bear-claw boots, and climbing equipment; excavation tools; bows, *bolas*, and my *atlatl*; tents and cooking supplies; a small *umiak* and oars; and all my wearable seal and bear skins. Everything that I might possibly need. Everything of a material nature, that is. I can't pack courage.

I use this clutter as a shield. Behind it, I am storing away the Boundary tools Lukas has given me, like my *ulu* knife. These items might be the difference between life and death in the first three Advantages. And then there's my journal. The Lex forbids journals: *let nothing be so secret that you write or discuss it in private.* But since Eamon died, I've needed a place where I can be my true self. In the past, I was able to act the Maiden—and be content with my role and my future as an Ark Gardener or wife—because I always had a reprieve with Eamon. A place where I could shed the Lex Maiden rules for a little while, climb the turret, poke fun at our mother, and engage in free talk. I could even whisper the banned Faerie tales I heard from my beloved Boundary Nurse Aga—like the one about young Maiden Snow who lays in a dream-state in an icy coffin, waiting for her Gallant to rescue her. Eamon begged for stories like these. This journal has to serve as a pathetic replacement for a conversation with my brother.

"What are you doing back there, Eva?" my mother demands.

I slide the journal and the tools under the largest bag, and meet her eyes to answer, "Just organizing my equipment."

She shakes her head, gestures around the room at the chaos. "Eva, all this must fit on your back or on the dogsled tomorrow. How in the Gods do you think you'll manage?" Her voice is at its true level, but she is no less the Lady in her quest for perfection.

"Don't worry, Mother. It's more organized than it looks. It'll all fit."

She glares at me. "I suppose I thought you'd still have the sense to quit now. In fact, I thought we'd had enough of your un-Maidenly behavior long ago with that tapestry business."

My heart squeezes. I should have known she'd bring up that embarrassment: the ill-fated mark that ruined my otherwise perfect ascent toward Ladyhood. On the other hand, she has a point. What had I been thinking with the tapestry? I knowingly deviated from the Lex-prescribed depiction of the Healing by including a symbol of the false god Apple hanging from a tree. Worse: with a tiny bite taken out of it.

In my defense, those few illicit stitches had been prompted by a secret Faerie tale Nurse Aga told me about Apple, a Maiden, a Gallant, and a Garden . . . and I'd lost myself in the beauty of the tableaux. The daydream-fueled stitching led to banishment from the afternoon sewing circles. The Maidens who'd been my friends forgot about me.

Instead, I began my tenure as an apprentice Gardener.

But not all was lost. I discovered that I loved learning about botany and agriculture from the Ark Gardeners. I think that irked my mother more than blasphemy itself: that I grew to prefer my punishment in the Ark to my time sewing and chattering.

When I don't answer, she continues. "Despite all that unpleasantness, you've decided to Test. Even though you're a Maiden."

"Other Maidens have competed in the Testing. What about Madeline? And Carina was given permission." I almost wish Jasper were here to back me up. While researching The Praebulum and The Lex—in an effort to prove that a Maiden should be permitted entrance into the Testing—I learned about two Maidens who sought the Archon position in the past.

"Those two *Maidens*—" my mother practically spits out the word, "participated in the Testing or the Commitment over one hundred and fifty years ago, when some females still carried the vestiges of the unseemly qualities of the pre-Healing days. Before they fully transformed into the Maidens and Ladies of the Aerie that you see today—women of The Lex. Madeline even trained with Gallants. Do you want to become like Madeline and Carina? Brazen and coarse?"

"Mother, you don't know what they were like—"

She raises a hand. "Enough. You've proven that I can't

stop you, but that doesn't mean I have to approve. You've managed to sway your father, but not me. Your place is here, in your home. And one day, perhaps with Jasper. If he'll still have you after all this nonsense is over."

And so it is as I'd suspected. I turn my attention back to my packing. There's nothing more to say.

My mother exhales. It's a sigh heavy with exhaustion, despair, and sadness. I almost feel badly for her. She's suffered over Eamon, too, and even though I jest to myself and Lukas about her ridiculous adherence to The Lex, I know it's her way of coping with her grief. I see her face soften, and I wonder if she might walk across the room to touch me. But then she hardens again into her Lady mask. As far as I can tell, all of my mother's gentle emotion—what little she believes The Lex permits—died with Eamon. Only duty and appearances and survival remain.

The door slams shut. I thought I wanted solitude. I'd longed for it all day, even escaped to the turret to find it. I relished the thought of finally relinquishing the Maiden role. But now I feel truly alone. I make myself imagine the next morning, when I'll stand alone on the town square dais with the eleven other contenders for the Testing. I envision the solitary departure from the Aerie, through the Ring—and the race out into the vast, white ice of New North, and onto the Frozen Shores. I might have to scale glaciers or descend into crevasses searching for artifacts, those terrible reminders of the past that washed onto New North's shores in the Healing. Then, if I'm lucky enough to find a Relic, not even one of the scale my father found, I'll study it in the isolation of my igloo. I'll extract a lesson from my Relic so that mankind will never again repeat its catastrophic mistakes. Only then will the Gods select an Archon from among us twelve.

The other eleven Testors are Gallants, like Jasper. Of course.

Deep within myself, I believe I can do it, despite my lack of training and the fact that, until now, everyone thought of me as a Maiden. Not exactly compliant, but a Maiden nonetheless. I must believe. Is that what Lukas always tells me? And didn't his insistence on faith in myself prove true as he pushed me to scale Aerie ice walls and learn all the types of snow by touch alone?

For the first time in days, I feel at peace. It is almost as though Eamon himself had given his blessing.

I unlace the front of my Feast gown to put on my sleeping shift. In the coming days, I'll not have the luxury, but day after day will sleep in the same layers of skins and furs for warmth.

The stays of my gown are tighter than usual, as demanded by the Feast, and I struggle with them. I consider calling for Katja, but I hesitate. Katja was chosen explicitly to suit me as a Companion, and yet I have never felt particularly close to her. She's nice enough, and loyal, but our relationship is nothing like the bond that had formed between Eamon and Lukas. That we all three shared, really.

A tiny knock sounds at my bedroom door. It can only be Katja. My mother is long gone, and my father's knock is distinctive and forceful.

"Come in. I was just about to call for you," I reply.

The door opens, and my throat catches. Lukas fills the room. Broad-shouldered and wide of chest, he somehow manages to make even the largest of tunics seem too small.

I turn around and scramble to pull tight the stays of my gown.

He backs away. "I'm sorry, Eva. I shouldn't be here."

As I reassemble my gown as quickly as possible, I rush to

reassure him. "No, no, Lukas. Please stay. I wanted to thank you for—"

"The turret? No need. I was just doing my job."

I am angry in spite of myself. "Is that all it is? Your job?"

"Of course not, Eva. You know better than that."

We stare at each other, uncertain what to say next. The Lex explicitly bars the kind of friendship that sprung up between us and Eamon: *let no familiarity pass with those of the Boundary; we are their caretakers, not their friends or families.* Consequently, I sometimes struggle for the right way to speak to Lukas. For me, this kind of free talk, unburdened by The Lex, makes me awkward and blunt. Even bold.

"Tell me about *Nunassiaq* again, will you?" I find myself blurting.

"I thought you were the storyteller, Eva. Not me." He's trying to put me off, referencing the times when we three hid away on the turret listening to the tales I respun from Nurse Aga. But I won't have it.

"Come on, Lukas. Please."

He pauses, then shakes his head.

"Eva, you leave the Aerie tomorrow as *upernagdlit*, not *Inuit*. When you make the Passage tomorrow, you'll enter a land that isn't *Nunassiaq* anymore. That place died when the floods came—excuse me, the Healing happened—and New North created the Boundary land for my people."

Now I truly don't know what to say. My mother would call Lukas's slip about the "floods" blasphemy, but I'm not offended that the Boundary people sometimes have different beliefs. Mostly, I feel sorry for them, that they don't have the comfort of our faith in the Gods. Besides, I have too much respect for Lukas to lecture him about the Gods-blessed events that led to the creation of New North: the voyage taken by the Founders to the Arctic islands that became our home, the manner in which the Founders banded together to fashion a rightful society when the Healing submerged most of Father Earth, and New North's sacred mission to avoid the mistakes of the pre-Healing world with The Lex and the Boundary and the Testing.

"Well . . . thanks for coming to say goodbye," I finally offer.

"Eva, I came to bring you something. Something you might find helpful for the Testing," he says softly.

A smile creeps across my face. I rub my hands together. Another Boundary-tool. I am not so confident that I don't appreciate the help. "So, what's the treasure this time?"

"A book."

I point at the bags all around the room. "I don't think I can fit any more books. My mother just informed me—as if I didn't know—that I'm limited by what I can carry on my back or on my sled."

"You might want to make room for this, Eva."

His tone has hardened. He pulls an unadorned leather-bound book out of the small bag hanging at his hip. It looks familiar, but then most do. Paper is a rarity, so books are reused and reused for Lex-sanctified purposes. As I stare at it, I realize why I know this one in particular.

It is Eamon's journal.

V

Martius 31
Year 242, A.H.

"Hand it to me," I order Lukas.

He flinches, and immediately I feel terrible. Even though I'm a Maiden of the Aerie and Lukas is just a Boundary Companion—making it within my rights to speak to him in whatever manner I see fit—I'm never so harsh with my friend. The hunger for my brother's words has made me cruel, but that's no excuse.

"I'm sorry," I whisper.

Lukas passes me the book but doesn't respond to my apology. I'm not surprised. He told me once that the Boundary people never discuss regret; they offer tokens to the people they've hurt. Instead, as if he can read my thoughts, he answers the question I'm thinking but didn't ask yet. "I just found the journal tonight, Eva."

"Where was it?" Since Eamon died, I've wondered what happened to the little book where he recorded all his strategies for the Testing and all Lukas's instructions. I've searched for it in all our secret places, but figured that he must have lost it on the Ring.

"In the floorboards under his bed."

Odd, I didn't know that Eamon stored things there. Clearly there were some things he kept for his eyes only. I palm the little book. Part of me wants to rip it open and gobble up my brother's words, and part of me wants to savor his last thoughts. I split the difference. Slowly, I crack it open to a random page and gaze at the familiar handwriting without absorbing.

"Have you read it?" I ask Lukas.

"It's in Latin."

"Oh, that's right." I almost forgot that Lukas can't read Latin. He can outsmart nearly any Aerie dweller in the ways of survival, but his knowledge has limits. The only Latin words Boundary people are permitted to know are those spoken aloud in the Aerie. The Lex forbids teaching them to read our written language. I don't like to be reminded that Lukas has any shortcomings.

"Will you read it to me?" he asks.

Of course, I say yes. Lukas never asks me for anything. I start with the first entry. It's not dated, but from the very first line I know exactly when Eamon began to write.

Today I made the Commitment. I've been talking about this day since I was four years old. At least that's what Eva tells me. But it was weird to actually write my name in the Testing Book and place it before the Lexors and Basilikons. To say nothing of putting it before Father, the Chief Archon.

Father always insisted that his role as Chief was fleeting, as it should be. Like time itself. He made me focus on what was important, not my privileged place in New North. Archaeology classes so I can properly excavate the artifacts from the ice. History classes so I can identify the Relics I find. Science and Basilika classes so I can understand how the Relics led to the Healing. And all this survival training with Lukas.

But somehow, the Testing seems to have come too soon. Will I ever be ready? Can I do what Father did? Should I even be a Testor?

I look up from the journal. "I didn't know Eamon felt that way. He never mentioned feeling unsure to me. Did he ever say anything like that to you?"

Typical Lukas, he doesn't answer me directly. "He didn't want you to worry, Eva. He wanted to protect you."

I shift on my feet, thinking of Eamon telling Lukas something so private, something he'd usually share only with me. I'd believed that Eamon and I told each other every secret thing. I was wrong. First the hiding place, and now this. I tuck the thought away and gaze back down at the journal. The next three entries focus on his training. The pages brim with all sorts of tips from Lukas on how to win the first Advantages: details about maintaining a dogsled, building an igloo, fishing through ice holes, hunting for rabbits and geese, climbing ice mountains and crevasses, and of course, reading the snow. Lukas had been relentless in his training exercises, and Eamon clearly wanted to remember every point. His life would have depended on it, if he had survived the Ring. Why did he even risk that foolish climb? Because he was unsure of his ability as a Testor? The journal poses more questions than it answers.

"This sounds familiar," I say, flipping ahead. "Do you remember that time you blindfolded me during a blizzard so that I could distinguish the snow from a *pirta* by touch alone?"

I laugh a little at the memory, even though I certainly didn't find it humorous at the time. With heavy storm clouds on the horizon—the kind that usually send New North dwellers into their homes and shelters—Lukas led me and Katja by sled to a remote corner of the Aerie. Then he hitched the dog team to a tree trunk, and waited. We watched as the winds mustered strength and the clouds darkened. Katja was terri-fied, and I was furious that Lukas had put us in harm's way. No matter the entreaties, Lukas refused to move—or explain himself, other than saying this was necessary for my Test-ing—until the snow hit. Only then did he tie a piece of fabric around my eyes, peel off my glove, and place the very dis-tinctive snow of a *pirta* on my palm. So began my education in how to survive outside the Aerie.

Lukas's eyes remain on the floor. "You need to be able to identify every type of snow. Even in a blizzard when you can't even see your fingers in front of your face."

"I couldn't have just closed my eyes in that exercise? I really needed that blindfold?" I say, taunting him a little bit.

He laughs. "I needed to make sure you wouldn't cheat."

"Me, cheat? An upstanding Maiden of the Aerie? Never."

"You're not like other Maidens of the Aerie, Eva," he answers with a smile and a low tone. Then he looks up and with a stronger voice, he says, "Anyway, I wanted you to be as prepared as Eamon."

"Am I?" I suddenly need to know.

He pauses for an almost imperceptible tick. "Yes. Just dif-ferently."

Before I have the chance to ask what he means, there's a rustle in the corridor outside my bedroom. I see a flash of terror on Lukas's usually implacable face. It's all well and good for him to train me, but if he were found alone in my bedroom, I can't answer for my father's reaction. The Lex would certainly support the use of the gallows. Aerie girls and Boundary boys are never, ever permitted to be alone.

We nod at each other in shared understanding. Lukas climbs onto my window ledge, opens the sash, and then slips out of my bedroom into the night.

VI

Aprilus 1
Year 242, A.H.

Only a few sleepless bells later, I stand on the platform at the center of the Aerie town square,
encircled by the enormous fiery torches lit for the
Testing's *vale*.

I've stood on this platform dozens of times before, alongside my parents and Eamon. Every Testing Day for the
past nine years, my father has spoken to the people of New
North. But this is different. This time the lit torches and
crowds are here for me.

I feel unmoored up here without Eamon. Everyone I have
ever known—Aerie or Boundary—watches. Not that they
have any choice; The Lex mandates the entire population's
attendance. I see two of my former School girlfriends—
Grace and Annika—both of whom turned their backs on

me when I decided to Test. Their scorn hurt only a little. My best friend had always been Eamon. My mother always lamented that our closeness prevented me from having many Maiden friends. Now, standing up here on this platform, I see something new in Grace and Annika's eyes— not only revulsion for my choice, but also fear for my fate. When they see me staring down at them, they turn away.

For what little comfort can be offered, I turn to my family at the edge of the platform. As with everything in New North, the crowd is organized according to rank: Triad members in front, Keepers and their families right behind, with the regular Aerie folk like Stewards and Guards in back of them. And in the far rear, the Boundary people stand, a nearly uniform sea of black hair and dark eyes.

Not surprisingly, my mother is decked out in her finest Feast dress, even though the Prime Bell hasn't even rung yet. She is peeking to her left, assessing the dress of the Triad wife next to her. My father isn't watching me either. He stares at the crowd instead. When he braves a glance up, I understand why. He can't conceal his own fear for me. The Lex forbade him to participate in Eamon's training, and he'd been confident for his son. Not so, for me. Maybe making eye contact wasn't the best idea. I want to stay strong. Or, at least, look strong. I think of The Lex: *let your children Test should they choose the Commitment, as Testing is a Sacred Honor granted only by the Gods . . .*

I turn my attention back to the platform. The eleven other Testors flank me. Gallants, all. Of course, there's Jasper, but I know the others as well. You can't attend the Aerie School and not be familiar with everyone your age, although we're patently ignoring one another right now. We are all wearing the same black Testing uniform: tunics over pants topped by inky sealskin coats. Gone are my long Maiden gowns and fu cloaks, and I wonder if I look ridiculous up here, dressed like a Gallant. I really have no idea, as I've never seen myself at length. My father's mirror Relic is the New North's best and most stark reminder of that sacred law. The Lex bans the use of reflections, so we Aerie Ladies, Gentlewomen, and Maidens rely on the honesty of others to get a sense of our appearances. That, and the occasional peek at a window or smooth stretch of ice. And I didn't get either honesty or ice today, other than a scornful look from my mother. Me: the would-be botanist, in my Testing uniform with my hair pinned up in the fishtail design favored by the Boundary women.

What am I doing up here?

The thought makes me self-conscious. I start to tremble. I have to fight to keep from losing my composure. I scan the crowds, desperate to catch sight of someone or something to stop the anxiety before it takes hold. At first, I notice only the tidy network of the Aerie town center—with its well-kept Keeps and interconnected, covered ice-bridges. Then, in the farthest reach of the town square, near the stone archway of the Housegoods Keep, I note some of our family Attendants, Katja among them. Her expression mirrors that of Grace and Annika; she looks both baffled and frightened. None of this helps my rattled nerves.

Only when I spot Lukas do I realize I've been searching for him all along. He sees what is happening. He mouths one word, the one he had uttered over and over in our training: "Believe."

I can't nod, but I blink hard and meet his eyes. I feel my feet on the ground again, solid. I stop shaking. When Father mounts the stage and begins speaking, I am composed enough to turn toward him and listen.

gather for the *Vale*, the farewell to our Testors.
men—" He clears his throat, and I wonder if
unintentional—or even a subtle encourage-
truly thinks the same of me as he thought of
Eamon. "Excuse me, these young *people* will leave the safety
of the Aerie and venture toward the most hazardous part of
New North—the Frozen Shores."

Here, Jasper's uncle Ian, the Chief Lexor, takes his ritual
place beside my father. I can't help but note that the deep
lines carved into his face are once more dark and frozen.
Gone is any trace of the celebratory Feast-goer I saw last
night. In fact, if I allow my vision to blur, my father and Ian
look very similar in their dark ritual garb, decorated only by
the tiny Triad symbol above their hearts.

"The Testors place themselves in the gravest danger for
the benefit of the New North people, to become Archons,"
Ian intones. "We of New North need Archons to show us
the perils of our ways before the Healing—the abuse of our
Father Earth that yielded the Healing floods. We need to
learn again of the hunger for Tylenols that poisoned our
minds; the thirst for Cokes that weakened our bodies; the
greed for MasterCards that toppled our rulers. All this evil
spawned from the worship of the false god Apple . . ."

I find it hard to focus on Ian's recitation of New North's
history and the creation of the Testing. I've heard it so often.
The departure weighs heavily on me, and Eamon's journal
burns in my pocket. Certain phrases haunt me more than
most: *I can no longer ignore the truth of what I've learned—*
and—*will they still love me when I do what I must* . . . These
passages are not at all like words my brother would have
spoken aloud. The twin I thought I knew so well.

"It is time for the final *Vale*," Ian concludes.

The Chief Basilikon steps onto the dais. He starts calling each of us forward to be anointed with symbolic Healing waters. When it's my turn to approach the front of the platform, I swear I hear a quiet hiss throughout the crowd. I know that my participation in the Testing isn't popular. Still, I'm shocked that anyone would be so audacious after the Triad approved my Commitment, especially since my father is the Chief Archon. I tell myself that I've imagined it.

Under the hawkeyed watch of the Ring-Guards, the people start to depart. They move toward that great rift in the Ring called the Gate, the only opening in the Ring.

There, all of New North will watch as we Testors gear up, mount our dogsleds, and ride off into the Boundary lands. I've witnessed the ritual every year of my life, but never imagined I'd be on one of those sleds.

As the people disperse, the three Chiefs give the Testors a final chance to say goodbye to their families.

One by one, we march down the platform stairs. I enter the huddle of my kin, and they pass me from aunt to uncle to cousin until my parents have a turn for a last embrace.

My mother, her face a mask of Lady-fortitude, goes first. Instead of hugging me like the rest of my family, she takes my shoulders in her hands. "Make us proud, Eva. This family has had enough grief." I tell myself that there's affection and concern underneath her façade, and I embrace her.

My father steps up. He wraps me up in his arms, as if I were a toddler. Into my ear, he whispers, "Don't worry about winning, Eva. Worry about coming home." He pulls back slightly and looks into my eyes. "Promise me that you won't risk your life to win. I couldn't bear losing my only child," he whispers.

I can't believe what he's asking. It's heresy to ask a Testor not to do their utmost: *let your children Commit in full. Do not hold them back with sentiment.* Not to mention that he's Chief Archon, a Sacred Guardian of The Lex and Protector of The Praebulum.

"I promise," I whisper back.

"Testors, it is time," Ian tells us, once he's loosened himself from the crowd surrounding his nephew Jasper.

I break from my father's embrace and enter the line of twelve. As we begin to walk toward the Ring, I'm thinking only one thing: I'm wishing that The Lex didn't forbid me from walking over to Lukas and saying goodbye. If I survive, credit will be his alone. And since his Companion work is over, he may well be sent back to the Boundary lands by the time I return.

We approach the Gate, and I see that the Gods have given me a chance. Lukas stands at the very tail end of the crowd. As our line passes close to where he stands, I break from tradition and wave farewell to the Aerie. But I look only at him.

VII

Aprilus 1
Year 242, A.H.

For the first time in my life, I make the Passage. Very few
Aerie people ever walk through the Gate; The Lex permits only the Triad, Testors, and Ring-Guards to take
the step. Now I see why. Staring out at the vast expanse of
pure white—and nothing else—I'm standing at the end of
the world.

I force myself to calm the vertiginous feeling and study
the landscape. Lukas instructed me on how this might give
me an edge when the *Campana* sounds. To my left, I see a
few small Boundary ice-dwellings clinging to the base of
the Ring. Obviously the Boundary people chose to build
these shabby, ill-made huts close to have at least some kind
of buffer against the winds and deadly animals that plague
the world outside the Ring. Beyond those lodgings, I see

only that enormous flat swath of ice and snow. But, from Lukas, I know to look more closely.

I squint into the brightness and examine the horizon. In the far, far distance, I spot the ghost of the snow-covered Taiga, the large forest of birches and pines that we are going to have to weave through before we reach the treeless Tundra.

It is this expanse—between the Ring and the Taiga—that I must know better than the other Testors to gain the First Advantage. I must understand its snow, and use it to my favor. And I will have only one chance.

At the Chief Lexor's signal, we head to the lineup of dog-sleds. More wolf than dog, my team terrified me initially. They resented me when I took over their training after Eamon's death, the only human to whom they'd grown accustomed. At first, the very tick I'd handle the reins, the dogs would snarl and gnash at me. Then they'd take out their aggression on each other and the snow would end up dotted with blood. It took me nearly a month to win their trust—and their deference—so that I could get them to work in sync and use their distinctive talents. By the time I har-nessed them to my sled line this morning, they'd become like the sister and brothers I do not have.

The lead husky, Indica, is distinctive with his pure black face. There's Johan, Hansen, James, and Singerneq, all hard-working white huskies, nearly indistinguishable but for the different placement of black patches on their bodies. The two grey dogs—Rasmus and Pierre—and the brownish husky—Akim—are good-natured, but will vie for position if not firmly managed. Finally, there's Sigurd, beautiful and black with a circular white patch around her right eye. She's the only female. A kindred spirit.

I check that my bags are secure and that the state of my

sled is in order. I give each of the dogs a rub. From now on, it will be entirely up to me. No more Companions. No more Attendants. No more father who happens to be Chief Archon. No more prying Lady mother. For the first time in my life, I must rely on myself.

My heart beats hard at the thought of what I'm about to do. I've never done anything even vaguely illicit before, other than climbing the turret with Eamon and writing in this journal, both of which seem like child's play now.

As I inspect my gear, I gather a small mound of snow in my glove. Rubbing it between my fingers, I see that the snow is *masak*. The sled's runners will drag in this wet, spring snow without aid. Surreptitiously, I dip my hand into the side bag Lukas prepared for me, and pull out a small skin soaked in whale oil. Under the guise of further examining my sled, I run the oily skin over its runners.

I continue to pretend to inspect my sled, but not because I've engaged in Lex-breaking. The Lex doesn't prohibit what I've just done; in fact, it doesn't address such tricks at all. That's because the Aerie—and accordingly, The Lex— grant no credibility to the Boundary people's knowledge of snow. But using Boundary skills in the Testing would not be popular with the Triad, who hold our fates in their hands as they calculate the points garnered in the nine Advantages comprising the Testing. Plus, I don't want to tip off the other Testors.

We finish our final checks and stand in front of our sleds, ready for the Lexor's signal to mount. I glance at the Testors on either side of me. Although I know them, I have no idea how they'll treat me out here, especially since Test rumors fly each year about betrayals and dirty tricks, even among lifelong friends.

To my left are Knud and Tristan. Both varying shades of blond, they always seemed bland Lex-followers to me. I recall being surprised when Eamon mentioned they'd entered their names for the Testing. Maybe their families pressured them, as they both come from Keeper stock. Or maybe I underestimated them.

Beyond them are Jacques, Benedict, Thurstan, and William. All four were friends of Eamon's and similar to him in obvious ways: gifted in The Lex but questioning, enterprising, and strong. Both Jacques and Benedict's fathers work directly for the Keeper of the Fishery, and I wonder whether that aligns them or makes them more competitive with each other. Thurstan, barrel-chested and more coarse than the rest, doesn't have that worry; his father is Keeper of the Grains, and he will have a place in the Ark no matter what happens out here. The same is true of William whose family has served as Keeper of Buildings and Homes since the founding of New North. He definitely seems more suited to the cerebral job of building design and maintenance.

Over the course of the morning, all four of these Gallants have shot me at least one sympathetic glance. I know that doesn't mean they'll be any less fierce in the Testing.

At the end of the left side of the line stand Anders, Petr, and Niels. I know each by sight but not well, other than Niels, who, not unlike William, always seemed quiet and bookish. Definitely more suited to life as a Scholar than an Archon. If I had to guess, the families of Petr and Anders pressured them to Commit, as both their families are fairly low in the Aerie strata, serving several rungs under the Keeper of the Flames. Their families have a great understanding of fuel and fire, however, so maybe they have an advantage I don't know of. And a victory would elevate significantly the status of the winner's family.

To my right is Aleksander, the son of the head Ring-Guard. He was always the perfect Lex-follower and teacher-pleaser at School. Yet, no matter how hard he tried—or rather, *because* of how hard he tried—he wasn't well-liked. He grins at me, but he's standing uncomfortably close. All at once I remember that his father voiced the strongest opposition to my Testing.

Jasper stands on the other side of Aleksander.

We haven't been near enough to make eye contact today; I'm not sure if I'm disappointed or relieved. Last night seems like a dream against the reality of the Testing, and I have no idea how to behave around him. Before I can decide whether it's wise to acknowledge him, the Herald raises the red Testing flag. The crowd sees the flag and roars in anticipation. We mount our dogsleds, put on our wooden snow goggles to soften the blinding glare coming off the ice, and wait for the final signal. For the only time this year, the *Campana* tolls twelve times to signify the Testing.

We are off.

I crack my whip in the air, and my dogs respond immediately. With the oiled runners, my sled skids over the *masak* easily, and I send a silent thanks to Lukas for all his instruction. Within ticks, I am alone on the vast white snow. I am in the lead.

VIII

Aprilus 1
Year 242, A.H.

When I was eight years old, the year before Father was elected Chief Archon, Eamon and I climbed out onto the turret for the first time in one of many attempts to escape Mother's tyranny. The Aerie and the Ring spread out before us, an infinite white. My Boundary Nurse Aga had secretly followed us, with a scolding finger in the air but an indulgent smile on her face; other than Eamon, my Nurse probably understood me best of all. Although I remember feeling scared of the heights, especially when the icy wind whipped my gown around my feet, I mostly remember feeling free.

Racing through the vast, empty expanse of New North, I feel like that eight-year-old girl all over again. Or I try to. I hold on to the joy of those memories, but the cold is already seeping into my bones. I can't stop Lukas's litany of instructions from creeping into my mind. What was it he said? Oh, right. Never let your mind drift because that's when the snow drifts in.

In those few ticks that I allowed myself to daydream and actually enjoy the sensations, the snow turns. No longer *masak*, it is the slicker, harder *quiasuqaq*. Suddenly it doesn't matter that the other Testors' sleds don't have the advantage of oiled runners. They gain on me.

I crack my whip in the air. My huskies respond immediately, but the other Testors are pushing their dog teams hard, too. Within a few ticks, I am flanked by three sleds.

Benedict and Thurstan charge ahead to my left—no surprise given their physical strength and years of training—but the scholarly Niels appears to my right. I resist the temptation to look at them. Instead, I squint through the slit in my goggles and survey the landscape. I need some kind of advantage.

The Gods smile down on me, the Sun in particular. In the land ahead, I see a change in the reflection of Her rays, something that I know Benedict, Thurstan, and Niels will miss because they wouldn't deign to have a Boundary Companion like Lukas. This change in Her light means that after a slight rift in the ice flats, the snow will become *masak* again.

I hook the reins and my whip over the handle bar, and scramble for my side bag. Pulling out an oiled cloth, I drop to my knees—a dangerous move even when the sled isn't racing at top speed. The sled jolts as we pass over an ice block, and I try to keep my balance as I rub the cloth over the sides of my runners. I hang on, but my thighs burn with the effort. Still, it's a feat I could never have attempted several months ago, before Lukas's training.

Before I get up, I take a quick look over at Benedict and Thurstan. I know I shouldn't—it signals fear of the competition, Lukas says—but I can't resist. Even though I can see only their eyebrows and a hint of their mouths, they seem shocked by my maneuver. And perplexed as to why I'd take such a risk.

Quickly, before we reach the rift, I stand back up and grab the reins. I need to make sure that the sled doesn't tip when the snow shifts; the oil will help only once we've passed into the *masak*. I pull back on the reins, not exactly engaging the claw brakes but directing the dogs to take heed.

My pack slows ever so slightly as we cross over the rift.

Then we re-enter the *masak*. I crack my whip again, even though there is really no need; the dogs are smarter than I am about the snow. They tear across the ice flats even faster than when we first started out. I'm guessing that none of the other Testors have caught up with me, because after a time, I hear only the sound of the sled's runners and the panting of my dogs.

After a few more ticks of quietude, my heart stops pounding. I'm pretty sure that I'm alone out here. But I need to be certain. I can't turn around, as the motion might signal the dogs to slow or change course. Reaching into my side bag, I pull out my most prized and forbidden possession.

There is a slight thumping in my chest as I grasp the handle of my father's Relic, the treasure that won him the spot as Chief Archon. It is a hand mirror. My father wrote a Chronicle about the mirror's vice that perfectly encapsulated both the sins of the past and the purity of New North. And also made clear the critical importance of The Lex's ban: *make no mirrors and let none pass before your eyes, as they are the embodiment of Vanity.*

Until now, for as long as I've been alive, we'd kept the Relic on our hearth and pointed toward the Sun. I am still shocked Father agreed to allow me to take it. My mother refused even to participate in the argument. But thank the Gods for Lukas. My Father, forbidden from participating in my training, saw the logic once Lukas explained what I could do with it.

"With this, Eva will have eyes in the back of her head."

I hold the Relic in front of me and move it slowly from right to left, careful not to meet my own reflection. I discern nothing other than blinding whiteness behind me. Not even the faraway shadows of Benedict, Thurstan, and Niels in the snow.

I have regained the lead.

IX

Aprilus 1
Year 242, A.H.

Even though the wind cuts through my sealskin layers, I allow myself once again to revel in the speed. I've never gone so fast in my life; I doubt that many in New North have. I wonder if the Maiden I used to be would enjoy this, or whether she would be terrified.

In time, when the novelty wears off, I notice an absence of sound. I can hear nothing other than the panting of the dogs and the whoosh of the sled runners over the snow. Compared to the Aerie—with the *Campana*'s bells and the town clock's ticking and the constant clomping of the Ring-Guard and Aerie sentry patrols—the Boundary lands are silent. It begins to disturb me. Why didn't Lukas warn me about this? He prepared me for so much else.

But if I stop thinking so much and pay attention, I realize

it isn't as quiet as I'd perceived. The air crackles with soft and unfamiliar noises—like bird cries and the shifting of ice—muffled by the snow. Maybe that's why the Boundary people speak so little; they need to listen to survive.

Not too far off in the flat distance, I see a slight darkening in the snow. It can only be the shadow of a frozen-in iceberg. These masses jut out from the ice randomly, a reminder of the Healing when so many Arctic islands collided to form our land. Based on the map Lukas drew for me, I will not encounter too many masses on this *sinik*. This word must become part of my vocabulary; it's the word Lukas taught me for journey-days or days-away-from-home. He gravely assured me that marking *siniks* might mean the difference between life and death.

Lukas guessed that reaching the Taiga would take two *siniks*. The trick to winning the First Advantage—the distance from the Gate to the Taiga—isn't simply to gain the most ground. No, the real trick is finding a safe spot to make camp before the first horn of evening sounds. Otherwise, a Testor can find himself—or herself— dinner for a polar bear. Food is scarce out here, and it happens nearly every Testing year.

My lead seems to hold as the Sun makes Her way across the sky. The outline of the Taiga grows closer than I would've thought. Was Lukas right that it would take two *siniks*? Maybe I've made such good time with my oiled runners that I'll make it in one. Or maybe the Boundary lands have deceived me and the Taiga is farther than it appears. Distances are misleading on the ice; I know that from the Ring wall.

It's also been several bells since I've last eaten, and I wonder if that's the reason I'm second-guessing Lukas. I pull out some dried fish from my pack and nibble on it to preserve my energy and focus. The unbroken expanse of white and the motion of the sled are strangely lulling. Lukas warned me not to let the lack of food and the landscape hypnotize. That could lead to sleep—which, if unprepared for—leads to death. Catnapping in front of a hearth is all well and good at home. But even in the safety of the Aerie I've seen what happens to those who nod off unprotected.

I hear a snap, and I stop chewing. It sounds like the ever-shifting ice, so I dismiss it at first. But then I hear it again. There's nothing unusual in the horizon, so I pull out Father's Relic and scan the landscape behind me. At first, I discern nothing other than blinding whiteness. But then, just off to my left, I spot a dark form on the ice that's too small to be another frozen-in iceberg. Plus, it's moving. I gulp down the rest of my small snack. Another Testor. And he's approaching fast. Where did he come from? I haven't seen or heard anyone behind me since I lost Benedict, Thurstan, and Niels bells ago.

I crack my whip. The first horn of the evening will sound soon, and I've got to gain as much ground as I can if I want to win the First Advantage. The dogs quicken their gait, but I see that the other Testor is getting closer.

I scowl. What would Eamon—or Lukas—do?

Unexpectedly, the grade of the flat polar expanse changes—downhill. My dogs yelp with excitement at the prospect of speed, and the sled takes off. My icy breath catches in my throat. I start to teeter. I'm in danger of losing control; Testors have been killed by toppling sleds in these exact situations. Pulling back on the reins, I command the dogs to slow. After resisting for a few ticks, they acquiesce, and the sled is righted.

The other Testor isn't so lucky.

There's a crash behind me, and I pull up sharply on the reins. Fumbling again for my mirror, I see his sled has overturned. In horror, I watch as he crawls out from underneath the cargo bed. I long to turn back and help him, even though The Lex absolutely forbids assisting fellow Testors: *let no Testor assist or align with another as the Gods demand that every Testor prove his own worthiness for the sacred role of Archon.* Before I have to make the decision whether to break The Lex or allow another human to die, a horn echoes across the landscape.

X

Aprilus 1
Year 242, A.H.

I have only fifteen ticks until the final horn. I must make camp wherever I am. Fifteen ticks to get to shelter before the polar darkness begins its rapid descent. After that, I am left exposed on the ice as a snack for any passing arctic bear or cat. I stop worrying about the fallen Testor, and start worrying about surviving the first night.

From my side bag, I pull out the hollow, double metal cylinders Lukas welded for me from scraps of a boat pulled out from the Frozen Shores long ago. I press them to the slit in my goggles. That frozen-in iceberg seems pretty close. If I push my dogs to the limit, I might just make it to the iceberg in time. Might.

The whip cracks too close to the dogs. I sense their anger, but the sound spurs them on. The sled hurtles faster than I believed possible, and I actually have to rein in the team as we approach the perimeter of the iceberg. I hear the long, low bellow. I've run out of time.

The air around me clouds up with my hurried breathing, mixed in with my dog team. But I'm also panting in relief that our journey's done for the *sinik* and we've found some refuge for the night. I dismount from the sled and give each of them a hug to thank them for their efforts—especially Indica. Then, as I suss out which side of the iceberg will provide the most shelter, I realize I'm not alone.

The fallen Testor has somehow righted his sled and made it across the ice flats. He now stands on the northern side of the iceberg, staking out his claim. How he pulled off this miracle, I cannot imagine. But I don't have time to specu-late. In the remaining ticks before complete darkness, I've got work to do. I must dig a wall of snow to protect my team from the night winds, pitch my tent up against the southern side of the iceberg, start a fire to melt water for my dogs— and, somehow in this seemingly empty arctic expanse, find food for them and myself. I'd rather not resort to my stores of dried seal for the dogs and dried fish for myself, because once they're gone, they're gone forever.

I'm dying to solve the mystery of the fallen Testor—who he is and how he got here—but that must wait.

THE TENT AND THE fire prove to be surprisingly simple tasks compared the issue of food. I can't venture too far from the perimeter of the iceberg. But a Bakery Keep with steam-ing loaves of fresh bread is hardly going to appear out of nowhere, so I push myself out into the black void. The lamp provides nothing other than a dancing circle of flickering light, a few footsteps in any direction I choose.

After a few ticks of finding nothing, I decide to give up and draw on my food stores. Just for tonight, I promise myself. I figure I deserve a break on my first *sinik* anyway. Before I pass into the iceberg's perimeter, I can almost hear Lukas nag me to try one last trick. Especially since his map shows that this is an area where game and birds might be found.

I close my eyes and listen.

"Ears are better than eyes for hunting at night," he'd told me. "Your prey knows that you're blind and isn't as fearful."

At first, all I hear is the wind whipping around the top of the iceberg. The low grumble of my dogs. And the ever-present crackling of ice. But then, just southeast of me, I hear the gentle flap of wings. Snow geese.

Very quietly, I extinguish the candle in my lamp. In pitch blackness I creep toward the sound. I force myself to trust in that repetitive fluttering noise and the specter of Lukas's words. The beating of wings grows louder. I can almost imagine what the feathers look like. Closer and closer, until it's above me and all around me . . .

I throw my *bola*.

I am rewarded with a screech and a gust as the remainder of the flock fly over my head. I run toward the commotion and, with shaky fingers, relight my lamp. A smile breaks on my face; I can feel sweat freezing on my cheeks. There, amidst a pile of feathers, lies my first kill of the Testing. Several snow geese, big ones by the shadowy look of them. Since I'm a novice with the *bola*—and I'm not even certain the *bola* is the right weapon for this target—it's practically a Gods-given miracle.

Wrapping a rope around the birds, I sling them over my shoulder with one hand and trudge back to the iceberg, lighting the way with my other. I make no effort to be quiet;

I want the not-so-fallen Testor to see what I'm capable of. He peers out from his side of the mass as I approach, but I pretend not to notice him.

I toss half the geese to my dogs, making sure one lands close to Indica as a reward for his efforts. As they snarl over the carcasses, I pick out one for myself, holding the rest in reserve for the morning. I clean my goose the way the Attendants taught me in the warm kitchen of my home, and place it over the fire. It's much harder in the darkness, even with the embers to guide me.

THE ROASTED GOOSE TASTES better than anything I've ever eaten, even the honeyed cakes the Attendants prepare for Feasts at home. After the bones have been picked clean, I am drowsy. But phrases from Eamon's journal run through my mind. Phrases I wish I'd never read.

Can I really survive the Testing? Am I really destined to be an Archon? Can I really do what I believe I must? This last question he'd written on the very last page, on the very last line.

Having survived the first *sinik* of the Testing—even nearly garnered the lead for myself—I can't believe that my talented brother ever harbored such doubts. If I can do it, he certainly could have. Not that I'm over-confident about my chances for the next *sinik*.

Unfolding the small diptych I brought in my bags, I kneel before the little altar and say a few prayers to the Gods. I stare at their gilded, circular symbols, believing that surely it was the Sun and the Earth who brought me through this day unscathed. The Gods and Lukas, of course.

My body aches in places I never knew existed before.

Just as the pain finally relents and I feel myself start to drift off, I hear a noise. Not the dogs, not the shifting ice, and not the wind.

I sit bolt upright, and grab my *ulu*. I fear the worst—a bear or a cat. Before I move, I listen again to place the creature. The sound is distinctly human.

"Eva, it's me. Jasper."

XI
Aprilus 1
Year 242, A.H.

I peek from underneath the flap of my tent, and there he kneels.

"What in the Gods are you doing?" I hiss. I can't believe the risk he's taking for us both: *let no words pass between Testors unless approved, as the Gods must know a Testor's full deservedness to be Archon by the Testor's acts alone.* If an Archon Scout should happen by, we could both be expelled. After all I went through, to be ejected from the Testing for a silly reason like a midnight chat! Still, I can't help but feel a little relieved to not be out here alone. And if I'm completely honest, a little flattered.

"You didn't recognize me?" he asks, sounding surprised. "You dragged your dinner right past me."

I blink. I never seriously considered Jasper as the fallen

Testor. All of us Testors resemble one another in our sealskin uniforms—except for me, I guess—but I assume that Jasper would've waved or something. Anything.

"We kind of look alike in our gear." I suddenly feel bad for not helping him. "Are you okay? If I'd known it was you underneath that sled, I would've . . ." I don't finish.

"I'm glad you didn't know. I'm fine, Eva."

"Thank the Gods."

"Yes, thank the Gods. But if anyone is going to break The Lex, I want it to be me. Not you."

I almost laugh. "Well, that's what you're doing right now. It's not worth it just to talk to me, Jasper."

Even in the low light of my fire, I think he looks hurt. But then he squares his shoulders. "You're a Maiden, Eva. How could I sit on the other side of that iceberg without checking on your well-being?"

I want to say that I'm not a Maiden out here—I'm a Testor, like any other—but I don't. We're both playing roles, and once again he's typical Jasper, a chivalrous Gallant even in the Testing. "I appreciate it, but as you can see, I'm doing just fine."

The tension breaks, and he smiles a little. "I figured, what with all those geese slung over your shoulder. Still, I needed to hear it for myself. And I have. So I guess I'll say goodnight."

He pushes himself up, and his smile quickly changes to a grimace. Bracing his thigh, he turns and walks away. He is limping.

"You're hurt," I whisper as loudly as I dare.

"It's nothing," he says, not turning around.

"Come back here."

He continues hobbling, as if he can't hear me.

"Jasper, please."

He stops. Pauses. Peering back over his shoulder, he stares at me for a quick tick, as if to gauge my seriousness.

I motion for him to come inside. Lurching a little, he finally makes his way under the flap of the tent that I'm holding for him. With two of us in the little enclosure, it suddenly seems too warm. Taking off my hat, I command, "Let me see the wound."

He shakes his head.

"Lift up your pant leg," I insist.

"That wouldn't be . . ." he hesitates, searching for the right word, ". . . seemly."

"Seemly plays no part in the Testing."

"But you're a Maiden, Eva."

Now I have the courage to say what I was thinking before. "Not out here, I'm not. I'm just a Testor. Let me see your leg."

Peeling off his gloves first, he folds down his *kamik* and starts to roll up his sealskin. Even though I've seen a boy's bare shin before—Eamon's, of course—Jasper's motion feels very intimate. Suddenly, the Lex rules for Maidens rush at me unbidden—*let no immodesty touch your eyes or thoughts*—and I cannot help but blush. My mother would die if she saw this. Or kill me first.

"I knew it. I've made you uncomfortable," he says.

"Don't be ridiculous, Jasper. I need to see your leg." Before I really think through what I'm saying, I blurt out, "I have remedies."

He raises an eyebrow at the mention of the word "remedies," but continues to roll up the sealskin past his knee. I have to stop myself from gasping when I see the deep gash in his mid-thigh. He has a cloth tied around the cut, but it's no tourniquet, something Lukas taught me. The cloth is soaked with blood. I'm shocked the metallic smell hasn't alerted every nearby predator.

"How did this happen?" The wound is deep and straight and perfectly formed. For an injury resulting from a sled crash, I would've expected something messier, with tons of bruising.

"When the sled fell on top of me, the knife at my waist got loose. I pulled it out, but I'm left with this," he says.

I reach for my remedy bag. My fingers are moist. All remedies and surgeries are prohibited by The Lex. Rightly so as they led to man's downfall: *let no man-made remedies touch your skin and no man-made blades open your bodies, as this allows the ancient wickedness to enter your soul.* Yet Lukas still stocked my bag with herbal Boundary remedies derived from Ark plants, like salves for cuts and scrapes. He showed me how to treat basic wounds. All Boundary people use such remedies, and many of them outlive us chosen. Lukas's grandmother, his *aanak*, is almost eighty— and she was the one who taught him such ways. So I relented with him, as I relent now.

I study my notes. I think I can help.

"Look away," I tell him. I definitely do not want him to see what I'm about to do. "And brace yourself."

As I dab the wound with a strong-scented oil to clean it, Jasper gulps. Even though I know it burns—and what I'm planning next will hurt even more—I have to proceed. A wound like this will turn Jasper into a delirious shell of a man if the animals don't get to him first. From my bag, I pull out a needle and start to thread it. Telling myself that it's just like sewing at home—that I'm sitting before my family's hearth working on a cloth for the Basilika with my mother—I hold the needle over the wound, and pierce Jasper's skin. I start to gag. I am lying. This is nothing like stitching a tapestry of the Healing. This is a horror.

Jasper cries out and moans, but I force myself to finish. I try to comfort him. "I'm sorry Jasper, but I'm almost done."

He doesn't answer. I don't think he can. I'm not sure I can.

Finally, after very nearly losing my goose dinner, I close up the wound with a knot after the final stitch. I wind a clean cloth tightly around the injury. "I'm finished. You can roll the pant leg down now."

Jasper's face is drenched and snow white. He shivers uncontrollably. But his jaw is tightly set, as if he's angry. He doesn't look at me as he reassembles his clothes. Perhaps he's upset about my Lex infraction. But, how can he be mad about that, when he broke The Lex himself by coming here tonight? Something else must be wrong.

"Jasper?"

"You must think I'm a coward," he mutters.

My shoulders sag. Part of me wants to slap him. Oh, the Lex rules of chivalry. Is *that* what's really going on? Am I really that blind? "How can you possibly say that? You weren't even going to mention your wound. And you even risked The Lex tonight to check on my well-being, when you're the injured one."

His cheeks glow pink; his face bears none of its usual Gallant self-assuredness. "I can't believe I put you at risk by visiting you. Injured. How idiotic."

"I can't believe you're out here worrying about me, when you've got a gaping hole in your leg."

Now his eyes bore into my own. "How could I not come over, Eva? You're a Maiden."

I feel something stir in me, but I don't respond. It doesn't seem right under the circumstances. This change in our roles has left me unsettled as to how to act and what to think. Jasper too, it seems. He pushes himself to his feet and lifts the tent flap. He is not trembling anymore. Before he leaves, he turns back and musters a tired smile. "Oh, excuse me, I forgot. Out here, you're not a Maiden. Just a Testor."

XII

Aprilus 2
Year 242, A.H.

Even though my mind swirls with images of stitching Jasper's wound, I manage to fall asleep. One of the benefits of complete physical exhaustion, I guess. I return to a familiar dream, one in which Eamon and I stand on the edge of the turret, hands linked. In the dreamscape of a crisp, full-moon evening, we glance at each other in perfect understanding, and then we jump. I always wake up before we land.

This morning is no exception, although it's not the end of the dream that prompts me to open my eyes. The sound of sled runners coursing over the snow wakens me. In my grogginess, I can only imagine that it's Jasper—who else would be out here before dawn?—and I almost call out to him. Almost.

A bright light—too bright and concentrated to come from any candle I've ever seen—passes over my tent. Jasper couldn't possibly have carried a lamp with that power. It must be a Scout, the eyes and ears of the Archons. They are omnipresent but usually invisible during first three Advantages. They mostly assert their presence at the Testing camp and Testing Site, where the last six Advantages are played out.

"Testor, show yourself." A deep voice commands from just outside my tent.

I move fast. Since I slept in my clothes, I only have to pull on my hat, gloves, and *kamiks* before stepping out into the cold. But the simple tasks are made hard by the fact that I'm shivering uncontrollably. What if the Scout had arrived bells earlier and found Jasper in my tent? Using remedies on him? Somehow, I finish dressing and stand before the Archon Scout.

The bright light, whatever its source, has disappeared. The Scout holds a common oil lamp before him. It casts a dim, yellowish glow on us both. Just enough to make him out. The Scouts are notorious for their tough strength, their unflinching devotion to The Lex, and their imperviousness to anything but the *nutus* of the Archons. Head to toe in black sealskin with matching eyes, this Scout looks the part. Except for the dark, almond-shaped eyes, which make him look like a Boundary person.

I do not speak. The Lex rule on communicating with Scouts is very clear: *do not speak before you are spoken to.* I keep my head lowered in deference to him and his role.

The Scout circles me for a long tick, all the while asking, "Tell me, in all this enormous expanse of ice, how did you manage to find another Testor to share this iceberg?" He pauses. "Before you answer, I remind you of your Testing vow of *veritas*."

I can hear the accusations imbedded in his deceptively simple question. That I am conspiring with another Testor, that we used outlawed means to find this iceberg shelter, that this Testor and I have some illicit relationship. I wonder if he would make the same inquiries had I been my brother—or any male Testor—but there's no way I'd ask the insubordinate question. It might invite removal from the Tests.

"It was coincidence, Sir," I say.

The Scout holds the lamp close to my face, presumably to assess the *veritas* of my statement. "You expect me to believe that your shared presence on this iceberg was sheer happenstance, Testor?" His tone is harsh, and although he is acting well within his rights as a Scout, part of me is surprised that he's treating the Chief Archon's daughter this way. But Jasper is right. And I've said it myself: I'm just a Testor out here.

"It's the truth. By the Gods."

He says nothing. He stands firmly in place—as if locked in by the ice itself—staring at me with the same quizzical expression. I don't know what possesses me, but I break from the rule. I speak without being spoken to.

"Sir, you can see that it's the only shelter out here. Any Testor who came close to this point when the first horn of evening sounded would aim for it. It's a simple matter of survival that we're both here."

The Scout's eyes are more piercing than the Chief Basilikon's on a Confessional Day. I start to feel terrified. For my insubordination, the Scout has it in his power to discipline me, even with physical punishment. Yes, even though I'm the Chief Archon's daughter. What in the Gods was I thinking by speaking first?

Instead of punishing me, he responds in a measured voice: "That's precisely what your Suitor—I mean, the other Testor—claimed, too."

Obviously, he doesn't believe either one of us, but I don't think that is the point of his words. By his Suitor remark—a clear, if brazen, indication of what he thinks of the Triad's decision to allow me to Test, that I'm nothing more than a Maiden awaiting a Union and I should never have been allowed the honor of Testing—he means to shake me. He might as well have said, "Let me send you home."

Under his gaze, I begin to feel even more frightened. Maybe it's the late-night visit from Jasper. It's not as horrific a crime as conspiring with another Testor, but it's grounds for expulsion from the Testing nonetheless. Maybe it's my use of remedies. Certainly its use would get me thrown out of the Testing, not to mention warrant punishment back in the Aerie. But I do not allow him to see me shake.

Finally, he delivers his verdict. "May the Gods go with you. But remember, it will be me—not the Gods—watching your every move, Testor."

I watch as he mounts his sled and cracks his whip heavily on his dogs; he's a cruel master to his team, I'm sure. I am immobilized as he departs. I've learned something valuable and unexpected, as Lukas promised I would. But I didn't foresee this: my sudden understanding that the Scout does not want me in the Testing, and that he will do whatever he can to keep me from success. And he may not be alone. Part of me wants to race over to Jasper and make certain he understands the Scout's meaning, but a bigger part of me wants to distance myself from Jasper completely. To protect him—from me and from himself.

Only a bell and a half remain until the first horn of mornings, so I busy myself. Even though I am trying hard to concentrate on the tasks necessary for the *sinik* ahead—on anything but the Scout, really—I'm acutely aware of noises coming from the other side of the iceberg. Noises that mimic the ones I'm making. The crackle of a fire, the whoosh of a tent pulled down, the growl of the dogs as they compete over their food, the thud of the sled being loaded.

Bags packed, dogs ready, I mount my own sled. The orange-red sun begins to show on the horizon, and I tighten my goggles to brace myself for the blinding rays, magnified as they reflect off the snow. I whistle for the dogs to get into place; movement of the sled is permitted before the horn for this purpose alone.

As we skirt the iceberg, I pass Jasper. Even though I'm trying hard not to make eye contact—the Scout could be watching—I notice he's limping only a bit as he crosses the ice toward his sled. I'm relieved my ministrations last night helped. But my biggest worry doesn't concern his wound. I'm worried that he might have missed the Scout's message. If Jasper plans on staying close to me, he will be caught in the Scouts' web, too.

XIII

Aprilus 2
Year 242, A.H.

The horn sounds, and I no longer have time to think. The dogs, trained to race at the very tick they hear it, take off. The *sinik* is bright and clear, and the snow is *mingullaut*, the perfect mix of ice and powder. The terrain proves flat and even, for now. My team is in their element; I simply let them loose.

Lukas's map shows that the quickest route to the Taiga is a direct northeastern one. The same route Jasper seems to be following. I suppose that either Jasper or I could veer off to maintain a distance, but that would require we speak. And there's no way I'm going to initiate a conversation with Scouts lurking everywhere. So we ride to the Taiga close together, as is natural.

Ostensibly, we ignore one another. We never speak, never

glance at the other. We simply drive our teams as hard as possible to the Taiga border, and, to my surprise, we are evenly matched in skill and speed. If a Scout was watching, he would have nothing untoward to report. Nothing in The Lex prohibits Testors sledding in close proximity. Sometimes the topography makes it absolutely necessary. But I feel Jasper's presence. And oddly enough, even though I can't speak to him or rely on him in any way, he comforts me.

The Sun continues Her progress across the sky, and well before She nears the horizon, we reach the Taiga. I cannot believe how quickly we've reached the borders of the famed boreal forest. The first horn of evening will not sound for at least two bells. It seems a surplus of time.

What starts as an occasional dry shrub thickens into a line of trees flagged by the winds, and then into a tangle of birches and evergreens. Intuitively, Jasper and I part as we near the Taiga border, taking slightly different paths into the increasingly dense forest. I stare in amazement at all the plant life; I have never encountered such verdancy anywhere but the Ark. I have entered a green world utterly different from the one I know, the white world of ice and snow.

When I dismount, I know I should ready my camp, as Lukas instructed. But the carpet of caribou moss glows such an enticing emerald that I simply must touch it. The apprentice Gardener in me—the one who spent years growing to love botany and agriculture in the hopes of serving in the Ark—cannot be denied.

Tying my team to a sturdy birch tree, I signal for them to wait. I wander a bit, collecting specimens of evergreen needles and birch leaves for Ark botanists and gardeners back home, as well as some samples of caribou moss and edible greens for myself. From my study, I know that the caribou moss will help preserve the artifacts I find, and that the edible greens could stave off scurvy and other nutritionally based diseases. I marvel at nine-foot-tall shrubs, willow trees, and broad-leaved grasses. A hare leaps through the moss, startled by my tentative footsteps. The thick moss cover makes it hard to walk, especially in *kamiks* more accustomed to ice. But I feel oddly at home for the first time since leaving the Aerie.

I wonder if this is what His Earthen lands looked like before they were submerged in the Healing. Or if they looked more like the Ark, where the humid air seems to breathe and every corner of Earth is alive with growth. But, unlike the Ark, this place is Gods-made.

I hear a crack of sticks and immediately regret my little stroll. What am I doing in the Taiga acting as if I'm on some Ark-mission instead of the Testing?

It's Jasper. He's walking some distance ahead of me, also without his sled and team. His stride is firm and surefooted; his wound has healed with astonishing quickness. Gently touching the pine-needles and birch leaves along the way, he appears as awestruck as I am.

As if he senses me staring at him, he turns around. He smiles, a beautiful slow smile. It's like those looks of delight one sees from the youngest children in the School. For a brief tick, my breath catches, and I forget why we are here in this magical place. I smile back.

But then, when his mouth opens as if to call to me, I shake my head. The smile quickly disappears from my lips. Before he can actually speak aloud, I raise my hand to stop him. I mouth the words, "We can't talk. The Scouts are watching me."

"I know," he mouths back. His smile grows sad. He'd allowed himself a few ticks of forgetfulness, too. We permit ourselves a tiny farewell wave.

And then we hear other voices.

XIV

Aprilus 2
Year 242, A.H.

"What should we do about her?"

"I think we should—"

Without waiting to hear the full response, and without even a final glance at Jasper, I hurry back to my sled. I pad across the growth, praying that I don't crack a twig and betray my presence. I'm initially so worried about getting caught in the forest close to Jasper that I don't think about the source of the voices. Only a few ticks later, once I've started the business of making camp, does it occur to me that no highly trained Scout would be so careless and unprofessional as to be overheard by a Testor.

Which of the Testors would be talking in the Taiga? About me, the only "her" out here? And why would they take such Lex risks? Were they conspiring? Alliances are banned—whether formed before or during the Testing—but they are not unheard of. In one particularly rampant Aerie rumor, a highly regarded Testor ensured a friend's equally respected quest for the Archon spot in exchange for a promise; supposedly, the two now serve as the Aerie's Chief Archon and Chief Lexor. Yes, my father and Jasper's uncle Ian. We laugh about those rumors at home, but other alliances have been proven and incurred swift punishment.

As I prepare my camp—digging a hole for my dogs, starting the fire, readying the water for the dogs, pitching my tent—I watch the forest. The Testors have to emerge from the evergreen thicket at some point. But no one materializes.

The first horn of the evening will sound soon, and I can't delay any longer. I have to reenter the Taiga to hunt. My dogs are fighting among themselves as their hunger mounts, and I can't afford an injured husky. Weaving through trees and underbrush, I return to the area where I spotted the hare. Where one hare lives, others must, too, I figure.

Knives, *bola*, spear, and *atlatl*, my spear, in hand, I squat behind the wide trunk of a birch tree. As I wait, I try to imagine which Testors would dare conspire. Eamon's journal entries contain assessments of my competition. He thought well of Jasper, Jacques, Benedict, Thurstan, and William—but only in terms of physical skills. He didn't think much of their ability to synthesize the past with the artifacts, a critical talent for the final, and most important, three Advantages. In fact, Eamon described them as "able but addled," even though they generally did well at School. He outright dismissed Knud, Tristan, Anders, and Petr as serious competitors, believing their parents put them up to the Tests; he believed they lacked the strength of spirit to win. The Commitment by Neils confused Eamon, who perceived Neils as a bookish type, and Eamon understood that Aleksander entered the Testing to prove something to his Ring-Guard father.

Nothing in Eamon's evaluations makes me think that any particular Testor is capable of forming alliances, other than Jacques and Benedict, whose ambitious fathers serve together.

Movement in the brush interrupts my musings.

I ready my *bola*, hoping to get at least a couple of hare. But it isn't a hare that appears from the woodland. It's a musk ox.

The creature is legendary for its ability to skewer a man with a single swipe of its enormous curved horns, so I fight against every instinct to flee. This one animal could feed me and my dogs for days. Its *qiviut*, highly prized for its warmth, could help me survive the long nights on the way to the Frozen Shores. If I can only figure out how to kill him. He could easily swat away my *bola* with a shake of his huge, shaggy head, so that's not an option. I don't dare get close enough to use one of my knives; not anticipating that I'd run into a rare musk ox, Lukas hadn't schooled me in the best way to slay one by hand. Even though the animal has a thick, hairy hide, my only option is my *atlatl*.

The creature stops to nibble on some caribou moss, and I look at it closely. I decide to aim at an indentation behind its horns. I pray to the Gods for their blessings, because if I miss, the musk ox will charge and gore me. Something he might have done even if I hadn't decided to take aim, I console myself.

Pointing my *atlatl* to the ground, I place my spear into the hooked end of the bone stick. Then I lift the spear and *atlatl* off the ground and align them with that spot on the musk ox's head. Then I release. I've practiced the *atltal* throw hundreds of times with Lukas—he thought the weapon would provide me with an advantage because it'd give me greater leverage and better aim despite my lesser strength—but I'm shocked at how far the spear goes and how powerfully it launches.

The musk ox falls to the ground with a deafening thud. I race to its side, breathless. My eyes are wide. I am shocked that I actually killed the famed creature. I want to laugh aloud, thinking of the absurdity of a Maiden from the Aerie slaying one of the mammoth musk oxen. But the thought of my mother dispels the smile.

As I examine the spear protruding from the musk ox's dense hair, still incredulous that the spear is mine, I realize something critical. Something that I forgot to consider in my haste to kill the musk ox. There's no way I can haul this thousand-pound animal back to camp by myself. None of the Testors could do the job alone. I need to harness my dogs back to the sled to carry the musk ox, and I need to do it fast. Soon, too soon, the first horn of the evening will sound.

Ducking and weaving through the darkening forest, I race back to the edge of the Taiga, where I set up camp. My dogs smell the musk ox on me, and it makes them frantic. They fight my efforts to re-harness them; they want to be let loose to find it. After a few stern cracks of my whip and a tick alone with Indica to set him straight, the team reluctantly forms its pairs and lines. How I'm going to control them and lead them through the forest without ruining my sled, I cannot imagine.

I soon discover that I don't have to guide my team through the Taiga. With Indica in the lead, the dogs guide *me*. They follow the scent of the fallen musk ox, and instinctively pull us through. I think of Lukas again: this is something else I didn't expect to learn.

The first horn of the evening sounds. Sensing my panic at the shortening time, the team quiets as I roll the huge creature onto my sled. I crack the whip as hard as I've ever done and we careen back toward camp. That's when I see them, making their own dash through the Taiga before the final horn. The two Testors who'd been talking in the forest: Aleksander and Neils.

XV

Aprilus 3, 4, 5, 6, and 7
Year 242, A.H.

hat should I do with my suspicions? The Lex mandates that I report any offenses to the Scouts, but at least one Scout is biased against me. Maybe more. If the Scouts don't believe my report—or even if they do—they could make my disclosure known and choose not to pursue the offenders. Sharing my suspicions about the Lex-breaking conversation, or an alliance, would then backfire, leaving me a target for the Testors I've named. And perhaps others.

Anyway, what did I witness? Was it really an offense as defined by The Lex? I heard—not saw—two people talking in the Taiga. Then later, I saw two Testors near the Taiga border. The assumption that they were talking to one another—about me—is open to challenge. And I feel certain the Scouts are looking for a reason to challenge me. Or worse.

The question plagues me as I ready the musk ox. From my time spent in the kitchens—watching the Attendants prepare food and listening to their gossip and stories, always with my Nurse Aga close at hand—I learned how to prepare the meat of almost any animal so that it wouldn't spoil. Even still, readying the *qiviut* and the meat is a job that takes me most of the night. I have way too much time to think about the Scouts and the Testors. I wish I could talk it through with Jasper. Or Lukas. Or Eamon, most of all. I miss him so much out here. Even more than I missed him at home.

By dawn's light, I have repacked my sled, fed myself and my team, prepared enough meat for several days, and made a decision. It's what my brother would have done, and certainly what the guarded Lukas would advise me to do. I will keep my theories to myself. I will no longer communicate with Jasper under any circumstances. But I'll keep a close eye on Aleksandr and Neils.

Other Testors—Jasper, Aleksandr, Neils, and Benedict among them—must have camped nearby, because we line up when the first horn of morning sounds. In unison, we immediately cross into the Taiga; we must pass through the forest to get to the Tundra, the final stage in our journey to the Frozen Shores, the third of the first three Advantages. When the dense tree-life of the Taiga requires my undivided concentration—I must stave off the splintering of my sled or the fracturing of my team—it is almost a relief. I don't want to think about anyone else for a while.

By the first horn of the evening, I have entered the Tundra—so white after the greenery of the Taiga. It is curiously beautiful with its frost-sculpted landscape, a treeless plain of ice and glaciers. In the distance I can see snowy peaks. And I can already feel the Tundra's extreme cold. Dread spreads through me—many, many Testors have died out here—but I push it down back into the dark recesses where the Maiden still exists, imprisoned. Instead, I force a steely determination. Lukas never treated me like a Maiden during training, and I will not act like one out here. I haven't so far, as Jasper can attest to. I will prevail over this. I have come too far to not succeed.

Rather than riding out onto the frigid desert to gain a small distance advantage, I cling to the shelter of the Taiga border. If Lukas is right, it will take me nearly five *sinik* to cross the Tundra, and I will need every tick of protection I can find to get me through it. For this night, I will allow myself and my team the refuge of the relatively warm Taiga. From the hum of camps being erected around me, other Testors seem to be making the same decision.

By the first horn of morning, I'm as ready as I'll ever be. Or so I think. Once I actually enter, it's clear I'll have to fight to stay alive every tick. From a distance the Tundra appears fairly flat, but really it's a mass of unexpected glacial outcroppings that threaten the stability of my sled. Frozen mounds lie hidden beneath the ice; even my experienced huskies break stride. I also notice that I am really hungry. And that my dogs are snarling and nipping at one another, the way they do when it's close to feeding time. Lukas had warned me that we would need to eat more out here, so periodically, I halt the team and toss pieces of the musk ox to each dog. I thank the Gods that I came across that enormous creature. Supposedly, according to Lukas's map, meals can be found in the Tundra, as well—foxes, bears, wolves, caribou, and snow geese—but I haven't seen anything other than a few straggly geese in the air. I can't imagine how the other Testors I spy in the near distance—Jasper, Aleksandr, Neils, and Benedict—will survive without the musk ox stores.

The worst part, though, is the wind. Growing up in the Aerie, I thought I had reached friendly terms with frozen air. That was the naiveté of a Maiden; I had no true understanding of cold. During the day of my *siniks* in the Tundra, when I must constantly focus on the dogs, the sled, the terrain, and the food, the cold seeps into my bones but doesn't imperil me.

At night, it's a different story.

Stillness in the Tundra means death, Lukas had cautioned. And I feel it the moment I stop moving and lay down in my tent. Even though I'm dead-tired, I'm scared to doze and let the icy fingers of the Tundra freeze me into a permanent slumber. I keep my mind busy to ward off sleep. I write in this journal. I tabulate the number of points the Triad might award me for the first two Advantages, if the Scouts return with truthful reports, that is. I kneel before my diptych, offering more prayers to the Gods. I lie back down and try to tease out the meaning in Eamon's cryptic, last journal entries: *Must we truly risk our lives in the Testing in order to be worthy of the Archon Laurels? Our lives are so precious and so few . . . Will they still love me when I do what I must?*

What did he mean? Will we still love him *when he does what he must* during the Testing? It's got to be something else. I even think on Jasper's words about a future together. Only then, under the extra layer of warmth that the Gods-sent musk ox *qiviut* provides, does rest come.

XVI

Aprilus 7
Year 242, A.H.

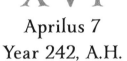

On the morning of the final *sinik* in the Tundra, I awake freezing but alive. Thanking the Gods as I bundle up and leave my tent, I learn from the howls that my team hasn't been so blessed. At night, the dogs curl themselves tightly and let themselves be covered by snow for insulation, but this morning, one dog doesn't uncurl. It is Sigurd, my lone female husky.

As I look down on her poor frozen body, I feel like crying. Sigurd was tougher than the rest of the dogs, but had a certain kindness to her as well. And she was the only female out here with me. I will miss her. So will her howling brothers.

I cover her body with snow and place a circular symbol of the Gods on top of the mound. Just as we do in the Aerie cemetery. As I tether the team to their lines, I feel like howling along with them.

At the first horn of morning, I have no choice but to forget grief and take off. I pass a rare patch of birch trees amidst the white, white sameness. I think how the Ark Gardeners would love to study this hearty growth, to figure out how they thrive in such adversity. Otherwise, the landscape lulls me. Dangerous, I know, but I can't help it.

By late afternoon, the ice changes color, becoming a slightly bluish shade. Only as my dogs draw closer and the blue grows more and more intense, do I realize that I have reached the Frozen Shores.

I stop the team from racing forward, and stare out at the endless icy sea.

I am hungry and exhausted. My muscles ache. My eyes and ears throb. I thought I'd be elated at the sight of the startlingly blue waters with icebergs bobbing, but instead, a curious emotion floods over me. Sadness.

Just as the Chief Basilikon said it would. Every year, on the annual commemoration of the Healing, he reads from The Lex:

In the eyes of the Gods, our world was corrupt and full of lawlessness. When the Gods saw how corrupt man had become, the Gods said, "We will wipe out from the Earth mankind whom we have created, and not only mankind, but also the beasts and the creeping things and the birds of the air." At the last tick, Mother Sun intervened and convinced Father Earth to save a chosen few. To those, the Gods said, "Make yourselves arks. Go into the arks and sail North. Take with you seeds and birds and beasts to stay alive. When the waters recede, you alone will survive to lead a new life following The Lex in our chosen land." The Gods then unleashed the final waters for forty days and forty nights, sub-merging the wicked and lifting the arks of the chosen to New North where they would serve as its Founders. This, the Gods called the Healing.

After he reads this Lex passage, the Chief Basilikon says that, if we should ever survive a journey to the Frozen Shores, the Gods will send us a symbolic gift. They will send tears to remind us of the Healing waters that deluged Father Earth in a rightful cleansing. This weeping, he claims, is the Gods way of telling us we are the chosen ones, and that they approve of our new Lex life in New North.

Icy tears pour down my face. But I don't feel like I'm crying for the reasons described by the Basilikon. I weep because I am staring at the end of the world. Billions of people and living creatures—many of them innocent bystanders to the evil that destroyed them—lie frozen beneath the seas covering the Earth. We of New North are all that's left.

My sense of sadness is quickly overwhelmed by my sense of pride and duty. We of the Aerie—the descendants of the Founders—*are* the chosen. The Gods have given us this one last chance to lead a righteous life. For me, this means that I must endure the hardship of the coming days—and win.

The tears crystallize on my cheeks. As I wipe them away, I notice a spot of red off to the west. What could possibly be red in this monochromatic expanse of white? Then it hits me; the color red can only mean the Testing flag. The final stop in our journey from the Aerie.

I crack my whip, and direct my team to the west. The first Testor to reach the Testing flag garners extra points in the first Advantages. Those points belong to me. Having worked so hard to prove that an Aerie Maiden is just as capable as a Gallant of becoming an Archon, it's my *duty* to win them. For me, and for Eamon.

XVII

Aprilus 7
Year 242, A.H.

acing across what remains of the Tundra, I aim for that spot on the Frozen Shores. The closer I get to it, the more wildly the flag seems to flap in the bitter, fierce *unalaq*. I also notice something else near the flag . . . a series of black smudges on the white landscape. What in the Gods are those?

As I strain to figure out the nature of the black stains, I unconsciously push my team even faster. Then I see: twelve Scouts in their black uniforms flank the Testing flag.

What a welcoming party. My stomach lurches at the thought of facing the Scout from the other night again. I almost want to turn around. The Tundra suddenly seems more inviting than that lineup of black. But I remind myself that this win is key. I square my shoulders, invoke my brother's name, and say a small prayer to the Gods.

Even though I've been schooled in humility my whole life, I can't keep a victorious smile off my lips as I hurtle the final distance to the flag. I've come in first. In fact, I haven't seen another Testor all day.

I engage the sled's claw-brakes, dismount, and tie my team to a spiky ice formation. It's eerily quiet and deathly cold as I trudge toward the black-clad figures, ready to receive some sort of commendation. Only then do I see that the lineup does not consist entirely of Scouts, although the Scout from my early-morning visit is present. And I miscounted. Jasper stands alongside the Scouts: the thirteenth in their perfectly formed row.

I nearly lose my footing. He got here first. How in the Gods did he do it?

The last time I caught sight of Jasper, it was the end of yesterday's *sinik*, and he was far behind me. Not a single Testor has been on my heels all day. How could he have possibly made up for the lag without notice? He appeared out of nowhere on that first *sinik* of the Testing, too. It's as if he's operating from a map I've never seen. A map that no one has seen, for that matter. Not even Lukas.

I know Jasper is just doing what's he supposed to. Still, it upsets me, as he's now won the first three Advantages. Have all his pronouncements—about me as his Maiden, about a shared future—been a ruse? Some kind of game designed to soften me? The thought seems crazy; I don't think anyone really perceived me as a major threat. Until we got out here, that is. Did he just play at being the perfect Gallant the other night at the iceberg so that I'd administer to him and salve his wound? He had no idea I had remedies, so how could he? I look at him, trying to read his eyes, getting madder by the tick. But he's staring straight ahead.

"Testor, join the ranks," a grey-haired Scout at the line's center booms, interrupting my cynical thoughts. I guess this is what counts as congratulations in the Testing. There are no extra points for reaching the Testing flag second.

I search for an opening in the queue. A Scout close to Jasper motions for me to join the line next to him. I'm still not sure how to feel about Jasper right now, but what choice do I have? To sidle up instead to the Scout from the nighttime visit? He scowls at me. So Jasper and I stand side by side, almost touching, but with a fissure between us. And not only because The Lex demands it.

Then we wait.

I guess we're biding time until the other Testors arrive, but no one explains. No one talks or moves. I pray to the Gods that the other Testors get here fast, because this stillness is excruciating. And cold. It feeds my exhaustion and general miserableness. Not to mention that my dog team is bedraggled and starving. Even Hansen and Rasmus, normally the most well-fed of the bunch, are looking uncomfortably lean.

I watch the Sun move across the sky, and silently count the bells. The sunlight begins to wane, and I think the first horn of the evening must sound soon. Maybe in a bell or so. As if on some unspoken cue, the Scouts gather at the line's center, gesturing for Jasper and me to stay put while they convene.

After a few ticks, they reassemble. The elder Scout announces, "We have made a special decision, although, of course, it complies with The Lex. You two Testors will be permitted to begin building your igloos, so that you may have some shelter by the final horn of evening."

How generous. We've been standing around for bells, and

they will give us a single bell to build an igloo. Of course, we also have to build a fire, gather food, and feed our teams. An experienced Boundary person like Lukas could fashion a rudimentary igloo in no time. Until today, I would have guessed that Jasper would need a full day for the task, but now, I'm not so sure. He's full of surprises.

Realizing that the Scouts could have given us the usual fifteen ticks from the first and final horns of evening to seek refuge, I nod in gracious acceptance of their ruling. Jasper does the same. We are dismissed.

Instead of running to tend my dogs, as Jasper does, I head to an area of the shoreline where a solid iceberg buffers the seawinds. I like the natural protection it offers, but it must provide a lot more. Lukas taught me over and over the importance of finding *igluksaq*, the perfect snow for igloo-building.

I take off my gloves and feel around. In a sheltered area just under the lip of the iceberg, the snow is too hard; it will be difficult to cut and won't warm up properly. Another spot seems promising, but the snow proves to be very grainy and won't stick. I am going to have to move some distance from the iceberg's perimeter to find the elusive *igluksaq*. Soon my fingertips are numb. The gloves go back on.

Pulling out my *iglu* knife, another gift from Lukas, I begin the laborious process of cutting snow blocks. My mind wanders to Jasper. Where is he building his igloo? Does he feel badly about beating me out in the first Advantages? And I ask myself more of those same, deeper questions again. Does he feel guilty about duping me into tending his wound, if that's what really happened the other night? He seemed embarrassed about showing me his leg, but was it a clever charade? This is silly Maiden-think, I tell myself.

I must refocus on the task at hand, or risk losing to Jasper once more. I should be asking myself how he beat me. Exhaustion has made my mind cloudy and weak.

I concentrate on stacking block after block in the round pattern necessary for the solid foundation of my new home, shivering with each painstaking placement. The word "home" sticks in my mind. The very word conjures up the aroma of hearty elk stew and bread cooking in the hearth. It reminds me that I'm not just freezing, I'm starving, too. True, this igloo will be my home for the duration of the Testing, but part of me wonders whether it'll be my last.

XVIII

Aprilus 8
Year 242, A.H.

arly the next *sinik*, Jasper and I stand on the edge of an ice crevasse, so deep it looks as though the Gods themselves slashed the Earth to its core. The Gods have not blessed us in the Triad's selection of this Testing Site. This particular kind of crevasse—sheer and straight down—is known to be the most difficult when it comes to archaeological digs.

The Scouts ring us, ready for us to Claim our position and descend into the abyss. Boundary Climbers stand behind the Scouts, ready to assume posts on the crevasse's ice walls. Their job in the coming *siniks* is to watch and record, but never help. Not that the Scouts or the Boundary Climbers will guide us in any way to the artifacts the Scouts believe are buried within the fissure; no, that would break The Lex. The Claim is up to us.

This is a moment that most Testors dream about: it's a huge advantage to win the first Descent into the crevasse. Every Testor wants to find artifacts in a chamber, cave, or on an ice ledge, all within the ice wall. Otherwise, you spend the entire excavation phase of the Testing trying to dislodge objects from the ice while dangling from a rope, something even the strongest find hard to manage. But for me, this moment is one that I've been dreading since I made the Commitment. Am I really prepared for a climb so danger- ous? Even with all of Lukas's training on the ice formations within the Aerie? Look what happened to Eamon.

I stare down into the vivid, blue chasm. It is beautiful in the sunlight. The large split in the ice sheet undulates in its descent, widening and narrowing unexpectedly. I cannot see a bottom, and in fact, one may not be reachable. Testors always return with reports of crevasses without ends. I try not to think about it. My job will not be to locate the bottom, but to discover a spot within the ice wall that hides artifacts from the time of the Healing. Or, Gods willing, a true Relic like my father's mirror.

Kneeling down closer to the edge, I study the patterns the way Lukas taught me. Down deep, the crevasse wid- ens on the right side, which might indicate the formation of a natural chamber. Maybe a chamber surrounding a large object? It's my best guess, and I decide to Claim it.

As I begin to stake out the area with the wooden posts specially prepared for this occasion, I hear a rumble in the distance. I stand up and turn to see three Testors arriv- ing at the Testing flag. Even though they're far off, I'm pretty sure it's Aleksandr, Benedict, and Neils; I studied them in my mirror often enough over the past few *siniks*. The circle of Scouts breaks formation. I figure that they're deciding who will record the Testors' arrival as required by The Lex.

Jasper and I wait.

In the commotion, I notice that Jasper is trying to catch my eye. I ignore him, but he keeps clearing his throat. Although I'm confused and upset with him, I don't want him to get caught Lex-breaking. I look around to make sure the Scouts aren't watching me, and I meet his gaze.

With his eyes, he signals me to Claim the left side of the crevasse. That side is coated with water ice, a frozen liquid flow of water. That makes it a more treacherous climb than the right, where I've begun to stake. Should I switch based on Jasper's advice? Can I trust him? Is he trying to help me or not? Before I commit to a course, I want to see where Jasper is going.

As the remaining ten Scouts encircle us again, he retrieves his wooden stakes from his pack and Claims a spot on the left side. Right where he told me to Claim. If I follow Jasper's lead, I will be ignoring Lukas's advice, which feels like a betrayal. But Lukas isn't here to assess the crevasse, and neither is Eamon. And Jasper's been training for this moment practically his whole life. I whisper a small prayer to the Gods, beseeching them to help me decide. Whose advice should I follow? Lukas's or Jasper's?

Abandoning my stakes, I creep around the crevasse again, studying the light and the ice in the Sun. Maybe She'll give me some sort of a sign with one of Her rays. I linger near the area Jasper has Claimed. For the first time, I notice wavy patterns in the water ice of the sort Lukas had told me to look for. Maybe Jasper is correct. And anyway, if I think about it, would Jasper Claim the more dangerous side unless he truly believes more artifacts are buried within its walls?

Still torn, I decide to follow Jasper's lead. I walk back to the crevasse's right side, and bend down to pull out my stakes.

"Testor, replace those Claim stakes," a voice behind me bellows.

I don't need to turn. I recognize the voice. It's the Scout from the other night.

Standing up, I turn around and face the Scout. Do I dare defy him? If I don't, I'll be stuck with the right side of the crevasse. I also know that if that Scout wants me to adhere to my initial right-hand Claim, I definitely want to Claim left.

The Scout spoke to me, so I can speak back. Voice quivering, I say, "The Lex says *let no Claim be complete until the last of the twelve stakes is planted*. I have only planted ten stakes, so it is within my Lex rights to remove them and replant them for my Claim." Not many Testors have scrutinized The Lex as I have. It was a necessary step in convincing the Triad to permit my Testing, but I didn't think I'd use that knowledge out here. I was wrong.

"That is not what The Lex says. In fact—"

"Scout Okpik, enough," the elder Scout commands. I am startled not only by his harsh tone but the fact that he actually used the Scout's name; Scouts typically refer to one another only by their title. Okpik is a Boundary name. I've never heard of a Boundary person becoming a Scout or even a Ring-Guard for that matter. How did Okpik manage to scale the walls that divide Boundary and Aerie?

The elder Scout continues, "The Testor is correct in her reading of The Lex. She is free to remove her stakes until the twelfth is planted."

"Thank you, sir," I say. Out of long habit, I start to bow deep in a Maiden curtsy, but I stop myself. Instead, I kneel back down to yank out my stakes before the Scouts change their minds. With Jasper's help and Lukas's guidance, I have made the correct decision, praise the Gods.

I finish staking out my Claim near the wavy patterns in the crevasse's left wall. Then, I unpack my climbing gear. I'm nervous, but I try to put on a brave show for the Scouts who are watching. Especially Scout Okpik. We are into the second three Advantages now, and every move will be assessed and tabulated toward their final judgment. Not that Okpik will be racking up points in my favor.

Removing my beloved *kamiks*, I strap on my bear-claw boots and my harness. Checking the security of the ice near the top of the ice wall, I insert my primary and secondary ice screws into its face. I loop my sealskin rope through the screw-holes and into my harness. We wait for the Boundary Climbers to belay down into position, and then, axe in one hand and rope in the other, I start to lower myself into the blue darkness.

XIX

Aprilus 8
Year 242, A.H.

My courageous façade crumbles as soon as I'm out of the Scouts' sight. I have never been so scared in my life. In the Taiga and Tundra I had my huskies. Now I am truly alone. Jasper's nearness in his own Descent only adds to the solitude.

I know I have to kick off the chasm's ice wall with the tip of my bear-claw boots to start my descent, but I'm immobilized with fear. What if my rope gets severed on a sharp ice point? What if I didn't choose a solid enough surface for my ice screws? What if I'm not strong enough to slow my descent and I end up in the bottomless crevasse? Eamon died on the Ring in this exact sort of situation.

Lukas warned me that I might feel this way, even though I'm a naturally gifted climber. Nothing is like the Descent.

He said that no matter how many ice climbs and descents we practiced on the bottom part of the Ring and the small ice formations within the Aerie, they would not substitute for the sensation of lowering myself into the crevasse's near vertical ice walls. I think back on his teachings. I take a deep breath, whisper "believe," and put the tip of my boots into the ice.

The kick back from the ice wall sends me flying down too fast, and I lose control of my sealskin rope. I don't have a powerful enough grip, just as I'd feared. My slight build was a strength in the first three Advantages—sleds race faster with lighter loads—but down here, it's a hindrance. Sheer strength—the kind hard-won by years of training— rules this phase of Testing. To stop my fall, I have to dig my bear-claw boots and my axe into the ice with all my might.

My heart beats wildly, and I feel like I might throw up. But I have to keep descending or I might as well head to the surface right now and offer my surrender—like so many in the Aerie want, including my mother.

I picture Eamon.

Using every bit of my strength, I kick back again and lower myself slowly down the ice wall, keeping a tighter grip on my sealskin rope than before. I think about one of Eamon's journal entries, one that seems to have been written for me, for this moment. *Never look up or down while climbing; pay attention to the present.*

Instead of focusing on the terrifying depths below me, I study the wall right in front of me as I lower down into the crevasse. I spot a patch of white ice, with its dangerous trapped air bubbles, and manage to skirt it. I avoid a particularly sharp shelf in the water ice. I identify a *qopuk* beneath a light layer of snow cover, and choose another handhold.

All the while, I look for some evidence of a chamber or cave or enclosure which might have formed around a large object when the Frozen Shores solidified in the Healing. Nothing.

Pausing periodically for a sip of water and a bite of dried fish from my pack, I map and graph the wall. That way, I will not waste valuable time in the days ahead by re-examining the same stretch of ice. I glance over at Jasper, going through the same exercise. I wonder if his heart is pounding as furiously as mine.

The ice turns from azure to sapphire. The Sun is on Her way down. The Lex requires that we return to the surface by the final horn of the evening, or stay down here all night. Something I definitely don't want to do. So I throw my axe and boots deep into the ice and begin the long haul upwards.

That's when I see it. Just off to my right, there's a grey shadow deep in the ice. Can I reach it on this rope? Or will I have to reposition my fixed line in the morning to get a better look? I want to examine and stake it today if it looks promising. Tomorrow will be more crowded with other Testors down here, and my chance could be lost.

Using my axe and boots, I claw my way horizontally across the slick surface. It's an advanced maneuver, a dangerous one that could leave me swinging like a pendulum across the razor-edged ice wall if I'm not careful. I reach the shadow just as my rope reaches the end of its tether. Reaching into my pack, I grab the *naneq* given to me by Lukas. The small lamp, he cautioned, was the only one I should use in the crevasse; a larger, hotter lamp might melt and destabilize the ice wall. With shaking hands, I light a flame and then to the wick. Perching on a small ledge underneath the shadow, I hold *naneq* close to it.

At first, I think the shadow is simply dark ice containing

the residue of some long-ago terrain. But when I hold the *naneq* closer, I see that a heavy layer of new, clear ice covers a large, inky form deep within the ice wall. An object appears to be imbedded far down in the wall's reaches.

Even though I know time runs short, I must lay Claim to this place. I take out four more Claim stakes, those that will mark the exact spot of my dig. As I carefully drive the fourth, and final, wooden stake into the ice wall, the first horn of evening sounds. I have to start my ascent. Dozens of Testors have missed the last horn and spent their last night on His Earth in a crevasse on the long end of a seal-skin rope.

I begin my climb back up, but I have underestimated my exhaustion. Each time I throw my axe into the ice, it feels heavier than the last. My bear-claw boots feel as heavy as the bears from which they came. The light grows dim, and the opening seems like it will never draw near. I've been counting the ticks since I started my ascent, and I don't think I have enough left to reach the surface. I don't want to die on this wall. But even my fear is lost in this numb invisible weight.

Above me and to the left, I see the bottom of Jasper's boots. He's closer to the surface than I am, but he hasn't yet reached the opening. As I watch him scale the ice, he peers down. And immediately belays toward me.

"Don't, Jasper. I can do it," I whisper as loudly as I dare, without alerting the two Climbers who are posted near the rim. We both know the penalty for talking to another Testor, let alone helping one. As long as the Climbers can't hear us, it might appear that Jasper has only backtracked. A strange choice, but not forbidden.

"You won't make it by the final horn on your own." He

reaches my level, scuttles his way across the ice toward me, and stretches out his hand. "Come on."

"No." He's right, but I can't bear the thought of ruining Jasper's chances simply because I don't have the strength to reach the top in time, even if it means I won't win. So I'd rather pretend to be annoyed with his offer of help and push him toward the surface with my refusal.

He stares at me, and says, "I'd rather spend the night down here with you than make it to the top alone. And I will do it. So, if that's your choice . . ."

Before Jasper beat me to the flag, I would have chalked this behavior up to his seemingly unshakeable belief in the Lex's command of chivalry. Now I'm not so sure. What are his motives in taking such a huge risk and helping me? Does he want to tell me something? Does he want to make sure I don't win? I really don't think he'd ever hurt me, but why is he trying to help me? Even though I'm uncertain about him at this tick, I have no choice but to accept his offer. I know what will happen if I dangle here all night.

I glance up at the Climbers, but oddly, neither is looking our way. Maybe the Gods are smiling down on us. Putting my doubts aside for a tick, I place my free hand in Jasper's, and he hoists us both up toward the opening.

XX

Aprilus 8
Year 242, A.H.

When we near the surface, I drag myself the last stretch without Jasper's help. Just as the final horn of evening sounds, I heave myself up and over the edge of the crevasse. I have made it. Barely. I lie on my back, staring up at the darkening sky. The Climbers were none the wiser.

"Rise, Testor," the elder Scout calls out to me.

My entire body aches, but if a Scout tells you to get off the ground, you do it. Legs shaking and arms burning, I push myself up to stand before the Scouts' lineup. Jasper is already on his feet. The Scouts don't move. Clearly, we aren't supposed to either. We are waiting for something, but as usual, no one tells us what. It's maddening, particularly when my fate could hang in the balance.

In a few ticks, the two Boundary Climbers rise up out of the crevasse. They walk over to the elder Scout, and speak in hushed tones. My stomach churns. Are they reporting the Lex infractions Jasper and I just committed? Perhaps the Gods hadn't blessed us with the Climbers' ignorance, as I'd hoped. Perhaps they were just watching silently, waiting for us to break The Lex so they could report it.

As the Climbers take their place behind the Scouts, the elder Scout converses with the Scout to his right. I hold my breath until he speaks. "The first excavation day is over. You may return to your camps until the morning's first horn."

I feel like collapsing. Out of relief that our Lex-breaking will go unpunished. Out of exhaustion from my efforts in the crevasse. Out of despair that I will have to go through this grueling exercise again and again. Maybe all three.

Instead of slumping into the snow, what I really want to do, I gather my gear. As I squeeze my ropes, screws, harness, and boots into my now-heavy pack—with the rumors of sabotage I've heard over the years, I wouldn't risk leaving them behind—I feel someone's eyes on me. I glance over at Jasper, but he's occupied with his own equipment. I look at the Scouts, but they are watching the Boundary workers tarping over the crevasse for the day. Even Scout Okpik is glaring elsewhere.

I'm about to chalk the feeling up to my imagination when I notice the Climbers. One of the two from the crevasse, recognizable by the shock of white running through his black hair, watches me. He doesn't break my gaze as I'd expect. He pauses for a long tick, almost as if he's making absolutely certain that I see his stare. Only then does he avert his eyes.

I'm perplexed by the peculiar exchange. Is the Climber

sending me some Boundary message that only Lukas could help me interpret? Or was he trying to tell me that he witnessed the Lex-breaking by me and Jasper? If so, why didn't he report it? What could be his possible motivation for protecting me? Or Jasper? I had thought it odd that neither Boundary Climber was looking our way at the critical moment, but I was so elated to get out of the crevasse that I didn't give it more thought.

The Scouts gesture for our departure from the Testing Site, so I'm forced away from the Climber and away from my speculations. In the dying light, Jasper and I tromp through the snow toward camp. For a brief tick, we're walking a fair distance from the Scouts and Climbers. Tempting the Gods, I risk a few quiet words.

"Thanks for your help."

"It's the least I could do. Anyway, you're much better than you think. Now that I've seen you climb, I think you could've done it yourself," he whispers back.

"I guess all those years climbing the walls of the turret are coming in handy." As I say it, I know that's only part of the truth. I'm stronger than before because I carry Eamon's strength within me.

Jasper glances over at me, perhaps surprised by the image of an Aerie Maiden scaling the walls of her home, even though he's seen me climb far higher ice walls out here. I sneak a smile at him.

"Do I hear talking behind me?" The elder Scout calls back.

"No, sir," Jasper answers.

"Good. I better not."

Jasper and I clamp our mouths shut. Being beside him is the most normal I've felt since I spotted him in the Taiga and we exchanged . . . what? A look? Happiness? Relief? For a brief tick, I want to push my doubts about him away and pretend that I'm an innocent Maiden again and Jasper and I are just strolling home from our School day. But I know I can't.

And then we reach camp.

Most of the Testors have arrived and they are busy establishing their home bases. Lopsided and crumbling igloos litter the clearing—only William's igloo looks halfway decent, and he's the son of the Keeper of Buildings—and I want to laugh aloud at the clumsy efforts. How silly they were to refuse to choose Boundary Companions who could easily teach them the art of *igluksaq*.

But I don't laugh. The Testors pause, regarding us, their eyes filled with jealousy and loathing. Especially Aleksandr and Neil. And even if a tick ago I had wanted to pretend everything was normal, I am reminded that I can't. I am reminded that my wish to be a Testor—and not just a Maiden—has come true. I know the price. This is a competition, and right now, I'm a threat.

XXI

Aprilus 9 and 10
Year 242, A.H.

I can barely sleep, and not just because I can feel the other Testors seething through my perfectly formed igloo walls. The puzzle of how to reach the shadow buried in the crevasse—without killing myself in the process—torments me.

My mind spins with all of Lukas's advice. I think through his instructions on snow, on climbing, on handling my huskies, on reading the icescape, on hunting and foraging in this barren land. But with the Descent, he reached the limits of his knowledge. His expertise lies in surviving beyond the Ring, not unearthing artifacts. Only Eamon can aid me now.

I pull Eamon's journal from its tattered, frozen hiding place in one of my bags. His words have haunted me since I left the Aerie, but I've had no time to revisit the pages. Carefully, I crack open the book; you never know what havoc the cold might wreak on its delicate paper. As before, the first sight of my brother's handwriting fills me with a strange mix of hope and sadness.

The book falls open to one of his last entries, one I've read and re-read. It's particularly confounding.

Must we truly risk our lives in the Testing in order to be worthy of the Archon Laurels? Our lives are so precious and so few. Sometimes, I put aside my concerns, and I let myself imagine a victorious return to the Aerie. Standing on the town dais with the Archon Laurels in my hands, I see my parents smiling up at me from the crowd. I watch Eva gaze at me with pride. The image dissolves, and I am left wondering. If I do indeed win, will they still love me when I do what I must?

What did he mean? What in the Gods did my brother plan on doing? What could he have possibly done that would have jeopardized my love for him? Didn't he know that nothing in the world could shake me free? Eamon was—and is—a part of me.

I push down the sadness and confusion, and flip back toward the beginning, where he inserted diagrams of ice excavations. I had no knowledge of this diary, but I remember well when Eamon worked on these sketches, a memory that embarrasses me now. The winter before the Commitment, he had spent the entire season poring through the Archives of past Testings, assembling a huge collection of summaries of past excavations, complete with renderings of Sites and details of the landscape conditions. When I complained that all this work left him with no bells for me—and that no other rumored Testor was wasting his time with useless drawings anyway—he got angry with me for the first and only time I can recall. He yelled, "Can't you see that this project might save my life?"

I didn't see then. But I see now.

Eamon and I made up, thank the Gods; I can't imagine if he had died with the weight of our one fight still hanging between us. Still, the irony hits me hard. That project I complained about—with such harshness and pettiness—might just help me survive. Even win.

I don't give in to the tears welling in my eyes. I remind myself for the thousandth time that right now I have to be a Testor first and a Maiden second; I can't afford the luxury of sensitive emotions—ever in need of Gallant protection—that should define me. Instead, I study the inserts. I pray to the Gods to find something resembling my Claim. Eamon included countless excavation scenarios—digs undertaken in trenches, ice caves, underwater, icebergs, and of course, the dreaded crevasses—but nothing looks familiar.

I'm about to close the journal when the last drawing captures my attention. At first, I had disregarded this page—entitled "the Johansen Site"—because the excavation took place in a subterranean ice cave, not a crevasse. How could it possibly bear on my dig? But when I examine the sketch more closely the second time around, I see that the Johansen Site is remarkably like my own.

Eamon wrote:

Johansen saw the black shadow of the remedies bag deep within the wall of ice. He knew he needed to extricate his rare find—undoubtedly filled with Tylenols and Ambiens and Prozacs—and show it to the chosen of New North in all its wickedness. But how could he remove it without causing the roof and supporting walls of the ice cave to collapse upon him? After praying to the Gods, a solution

came to him. Johansen would slowly melt the ice by means of a small fire, siphon the water outside the cave, and then allow the walls to harden overnight so they would not fall down upon him—with the frame of a wooden scaffold underneath the ice for support.

That's exactly what I would have to do. Johansen came up with an ingenious solution, and Eamon copied his explicit diagrams. Johansen must have been successful, because he was named Archon his year.

I thank the Gods . . . and Eamon.

Grabbing the grid I'd mapped out earlier that *sinik*, I spend the remaining bells of the night coming up with a design based on Johansen's plan. It will take extra ticks and extra effort, but I think it will work. I just hope that the artifact within the grey shadow is worth it. A worthy Relic.

By morning, I'm prepared. After I've eaten and dressed, I spend a little time with my dogs; I don't want our bond to weaken. I rub each one down, and then feed and water them before hitching them to their ropes. Watching the other Testors rush to form a line before the first horn, I feel their apprehension to reach the Site. So do their dog teams; their huskies are barking and nipping at one another.

I need to be on the southernmost end of the line, so I'm in no hurry to fall in with the other Testors. In fact, I need to join the line last to secure the perfect spot. My hesitation seems to make the other Testors even more anxious; they keep looking over at me, mystified that I'm not dashing over to them. When it appears as though all nine Testors who reached the camp have entered the line—I haven't seen Tristan and Anders yet, and I counted only ten igloos—I pull my sled into formation.

I slide into place next to Jacques, who greets me with a cordial nod. Other Testors—Knud, Benedict, Thurstan,

William, Petr, Aleksandr, and especially Niels—glare at me. I am the enemy, even though some of them were close to Eamon, too. Jasper sneaks me a tiny smile before climbing on his sled.

The air is thick with our exhaled breath. It seems like endless ticks before the Scout places the horn to his lips. When the first horn of morning finally reverberates, the Testors crack their whips and take off north toward the Testing Site.

All except me.

XXII

Aprilus 10
Year 242, A.H.

I break ranks and head due south. In order to extract the artifact safely from my Claim, I need to build a scaffold and, for that, I need wood. *Wood.* Out here, in the treeless Tundra. It's almost laughable.

All my hopes are pinned on the small patch of birch trees that I spotted on my way to the Testing flag. I whisper a small prayer to the Gods that I properly recall the trees' location. Otherwise, I could spend *siniks* out here searching. I don't have *siniks* to spare.

Nearly two bells from the first horn, I see a tiny smudge in the whiteness of the Tundra. Could it really be the trees? It might as easily be a resting animal pack, a flock of snow geese, or a frozen-in iceberg. Pulling out the welded metal tubes Lukas made me, I push up my goggles and press the tubes close to my eyes. The outline of the birches is unmistakable.

Although I want to let out a whoop of excitement, I don't want to scare my team. I whistle to them instead, and the sled picks up speed. A few ticks later, I am counting my blessings when I hear the distinctive sound of another sled's runners coursing over the snow. Who else could be out here? Suddenly, I think of Jasper, and I pray that he hasn't risked his chances to follow me. And my chances too.

Sliding out my mirror from the side bag, I don't see Jasper in my wake. What I do see makes me wish Jasper had trailed me into the Tundra: a pair of Scouts. They motion for me to halt. I engage the claw-brakes, and stop my team's eager progress. Hiding my mirror as I dismount, I stand to face the elder Scout and Scout Okpik. I'm not shocked that Okpik wanted to track me down, but I'm surprised to see that he dragged the elder Scout along with him.

"Are you Forsaking, Testor?" the elder Scout asks.

"No, sir. I am not Forsaking my Commitment," I say.

"Then, what in the Gods are you doing out here in the Tundra?" he demands.

"I am gathering wood, sir," I say, even though I know it sounds ridiculous. What else can I offer up? It's the truth.

"Wood?"

"Yes, sir. Wood."

"In the Tundra?"

"Yes, sir. It's just to the south." I gesture toward the patch of birch trees. When they don't say anything else, I babble into the silence, "Sir, The Lex says—"

Scout Okpik interrupts me. "I don't want to hear anymore of your Lex quotes to cover up your lies. Why would you leave behind a fully staked-out Claim? Are you meeting someone out here?"

The elder Scout shoots him a glance. "Testor, you have the right to leave the Testing camp and Site to acquire materials for your dig. It is uncommon to do so, but you are correct that The Lex allows it. You have declared your intention. We will watch while you proceed."

I can't help but smile. Scout Okpik seethes, but he cedes to his superior. The Scouts' oath requires obedience, or *pareo*. They stand by as I mount my sled, and I hear them follow as I take off toward the trees.

We dismount near the birches. The Scouts stand by as I hoist my heavy axe into the air. I wince in embarrassment, missing the trunk with my first swing. Even though I hit my mark with the next attempts, it feels strange and awkward to have the Scouts watch idly as I struggle to fell the birches and split their thick trunks. If we were in the Aerie, they'd rush to help Eva the Maiden. Or they'd think I'd gone insane. Or both.

When we return to the Testing Site almost five bells from the first horn of morning, I do my best to pretend that I don't have a Scout escort. Some of the other Testors sit or stand near the crevasse as they break for food, and I refuse to meet their inquisitive gazes as I dismount. I hold my head high, put on my climbing gear, and strap my packet of wood onto my back. As I do, I notice that Scout Okpik is standing next to Aleksandr, watching me. I swear I see their mouths move, quietly whispering to each other. What in the Gods are those two talking about? What secrets do they share?

I shake off my suspicions and descend into my Claim. I won't allow myself to become distracted. Even though I've tied the wood into the smallest bundle possible, the extra weight makes it hard to control my descent at first. I dig my boots and axe into the crevasse wall, and grip onto my sealskin rope with all my strength. In a few ticks, I establish a rhythm, and soon I reach my Testing stakes.

As I harness into place and light my *naneq*, I allow myself a glimpse upward. I spot Jasper above me and to the right, and I see the bottoms of two unfamiliar pair of boots above me and to the left. All three Testors are strapped into their ropes and digging hard with their pickaxes. There might be a few Testors below me, but I've learned not to look down. And I try to ignore the presence of the Climbers.

Holding my *naneq* close to the ice wall, I'm almost afraid at what I'll find, or rather what I won't. What if the grey shadow is just that—a shadow? What if I haven't located an artifact, and all I've managed to do over the past *sinik* and a half is enrage the Scouts and waste precious ticks?

Inhaling deeply, I place the *naneq* as closely as I dare to the ice. At first, all I can perceive is the wavy, outer layer—the *nutaaq*. Realizing that I'm holding the *naneq* too close to distinguish the inner layers, I pull the light away from the crevasse wall. Only then can I discern the outlines of the grey shadow quite clearly.

I swear it's the outline of a body.

XXIII
Aprilus 10
Year 242, A.H.

Instinctively, I recoil. I know I should be thrilled to see a two-hundred-and-fifty-year-old body frozen in a crevasse—that's why I'm out here, after all—but I fly off the ice wall, and sway out into the air. When I swing back, I crash right into the area where I saw the face. I brace myself for a closer look, but when I stare right at the spot, the face has disappeared. All I can make out is the grey shadow.

Was the shape of a body just a trick of the light?

Even though I can't perceive the precise outline of a body again—no matter the angle of the *naneq*—I'm excited. Whatever is buried in the ice wall of my Claim, I have definitely discovered a Relic.

Energized, I hitch the *naneq* to one of my stakes and pull Eamon's diagram out of my pack. Using my pick,

I map out my design in the wall. Then I start unloading the wood from my pack and hammering the initial frame of my scaffold into place. By the time the light darkens, I have managed to hollow out an area behind the frame. In the morning I'll be ready to begin the difficult work of excavation.

Well before the first horn of evening sounds, I start to haul my way to the surface. I don't want to get stuck like I nearly did yesterday. Although I struggle with the climb, I remember that I have Eamon within me, too. I manage to reach the top of the crevasse just as the first horn blows. When I emerge, the air is *nittaalaq*, thick with snow. The Gods-blessed days of Sun are over. I hope Their blessings haven't left with Her.

Once all the Testors emerge from the crevasse, we follow the Boundary Climbers and the Scouts back to camp. I can only see a few hands-breadth in front of me. When we reach the clearing, other Boundary workers have lit a communal fire. Snowflakes melt in midair. I can see the fish roasting over the flames. The Lex provides that, once the Testors have proven their mettle in the wild through the first three Advantages, they need only focus on the archaeological excavation and the Chronicles at the Site. Having had my food prepared for me all my life, I didn't know just how much I'd appreciate it once I reached the Site. It feels almost decadent having someone else find food and prepare it for me. I'll never take the Attendants at home for granted again, if I get the chance to be indulged by them once more.

At the elder Scout's signal, we Testors head toward seal-skin mats laid around the crackling blaze. I look around for Jasper. My gaze sweeps over the other Testors, all of whom look exhausted and thin. They didn't have the benefit of the musk ox during their journey. Then, I see Jasper behind them, moving toward a sealskin mat. In comparison, he doesn't look quite as gaunt.

When the Boundary workers serve the fish over a grain-root vegetable mix, we all devour it. When we finish this silent meal, the elder Scout stands and motions for us to rise, too. I assume that he's going to release us back to our respective igloos. Instead, he raises his hands to the sky in supplication.

"We offer a prayer to the Gods for our brothers Tristan and Anders. When Testors Tristan and Anders did not make camp last evening as expected, Scouts went out in search for them. Her light of morning revealed that our brother Tristan surrendered to the icy grip of the Tundra—caught in a barren area at the final horn of evening. Her morning Sunlight also made plain that our brother Anders met a similar fate, though the Tundra's wild creatures trapped him in their grips before the cold did. While we lament the loss of our brothers, we know that the Gods will welcome Tristan and Anders into their realm. For they lost their lives in the sacred trial of the Testing, which the Gods themselves sanctified in The Lex for the good of mankind after the Healing. We raise our hands in prayer for Tristan and Anders."

Tristan and Anders. Gone. I feel sick. Their deaths bring back the terrible moment when the Ring-Guards brought Eamon's broken body to our home. I don't remember much about the bells that followed on that awful day, but I do recall falling to my knees and letting out an instinctive, keening cry. And I remember my parents' crumpling to the floor, too. Sobbing over Eamon's lifeless face. How will Tristan and Anders' poor parents react when the Scouts deliver their sons' maimed bodies to their doorsteps? Will they remain brave and stoic at that moment—and the funeral in the Aerie's cemetery—because their sons "lost their lives in a sacred trial" like the elder Scout said? Or will they fume like I did, before I shut it all down to come out here?

I raise my hands as the Scout instructs. But instead of gazing up at the sky as The Lex demands, I sneak another look at the remaining Testors. I really take them in—not just as a Maiden in the Aerie would look at a Gallant, or as one Testor would size up another—but as fellow human beings.

Most everyone looks sad and scared. The hard reality of the Testing has just hit them. Knud is crying as he stares up at the heavens. Tristan was one of his closest friends; I never recall seeing one without the other. In fact, they were so inseparable at School that we nicknamed them "the Flaxen twins." I didn't know Anders that well; he kept to himself. Still, I have a very clear memory of his face shining with pride when he answered one of Teacher's most challenging Healing-history questions. Maybe it was this interest in Healing scholarship that possessed him to brave the Testing.

In the firelight, tears glisten on other cheeks—those of Jacques, Benedict, William, Thurstan, and Jasper. But I don't see tears on Aleksandr or Neils. Aleksandr actually looks stony. And I can't cry, either. Why? At first I think it's because I wasn't particularly close to either one, but then I realize that I've already suffered the most unimaginable loss. Why in the Gods did Eamon have to take on the foolish challenge of the Ring summit, and abandon me to all this?

Instead of tears, rage kindles inside me. These young men are some of the very last people left on this Earth, and they are risking their lives for the Testing. Human-kind clings so precariously to the surface of the world;

why would the leaders of New North subject its brightest and best to a competition that kills without fail, every year? Why must the Archon Laurels be so dearly won? I know The Lex tells us that in order to win the Archon honor we must risk our lives, as our Founding ancestors did, so that the memory of the Healing never dies. We are humankind's last hope for survival, after all. Still, it seems that our lives—all lives, in fact—should be cherished and protected.

Is that what my brother meant when he asked: *Must we truly risk our lives in the Testing in order to be worthy of the Archon Laurels? Our lives are so precious and so few . . . Will they still love me when I do what I must?*

Do what he must? Did he mean to change the Testing?

XXIV

Aprilus 11, 12, 13, 14, 15, and 16
Year 242, A.H.

A s I head back to my igloo for the night, I promise myself that I will solve the riddle of Eamon's words when I return home to the Aerie. I kneel before my diptych and pray to the Gods for relief from my doubts and for sleep, but neither comes.

I keep imagining myself wearing the circular wreath of the Laurels—just like Eamon wrote—and I wonder what Eamon would really think if he saw me now. I took on the mantle of the Testing because I believed it was his dream. But isn't this exactly what he didn't want? Me, out here?

I write all my secret thoughts down in this journal. I can't fall asleep. Images of Tristan and Anders haunt me. I picture their eager, hopeful faces as they mounted their sleds at the Passage and plowed through the snow drifts. And memories of Eamon replay in my mind. All casualties of the Testing.

Finally I doze, and even though I wake up anything but refreshed the next morning, I am determined. I will pursue this Johansen Site strategy. I will not be lost to these rituals. At the first horn, I will race to my Claim and do everything possible to unearth a Relic from the ice. I will give purpose to the sacrifices of Tristan and Anders in addition to Eamon. Even if I'm right that he did question the Testing—or more.

I KEEP MY VOW, but my artifacts are not so keen to be extricated from their icy grave. Bit by painful bit, I dig into the ice to erect more scaffolding, melt down a thin layer of ice, and siphon the runoff down a tube to the crevasse below so that it won't refreeze in the night. Just like Johansen did. Then I do it all over again.

By the first horn of evening, all I've accomplished is creating a small hollow in the side of the crevasse.

And so I spend the better part of six *siniks* burrowing into the ice wall in this maddening manner. Yet the artifact refuses to reveal itself. Every time I think I'm getting closer—and that the elusive grey shadow is taking form—I find myself up against another layer of ice. Each evening, I return to my igloo empty-handed. Only to face another sleep-deprived night, filled with visions of Eamon and Tristan and Anders.

By midday on the sixth *sinik*—exhausted but at least well-fed—I begin to doubt my strategy. The frozen stale air around me is loud with other Testors calling out for Boundary Climbers to witness their Relics. Lex protocol demands a Climber witness the actual removal of an artifact from the Claim in order for the item to be considered a Relic for the Testing.

The crevasse's ice wall has begun to crawl with Testors and Boundary Climbers and new ropes and pulleys to carry the Relics to the surface. I catch snatches of whispered conversations between Testors and Climbers. Funny how the structure of the crevasse allows me to hear discussions on the far side of the ice wall, yet discussions taking place right above me remain inaudible. Not funny at all, actually. This strange phenomenon means that I can't figure out what Jasper found even though he's dangling directly overheard, yet I can hear quite clearly the conversation among Aleksandr, Neils, and a Climber about their shared discovery of a large cache of weapons—the Tech called "guns"—that the pre-Healing people used for their destructive wars. Gun Relics are always hugely popular finds, as they are almost always of a different breed, and they often lead to an Archon victory. Learning this doesn't exactly help my mood.

With every overheard whisper, with every gobbled-down meal over the communal fire, with every Testor's race back to his igloo to study his Relic under the gaze of a Scout serving as Reliquon, I get more and more upset. The Scout-Reliquons are the Relic keepers. I imagine the carrier pigeons landing in the Aerie town square, carrying initial reports of the Relics in the tiny packs around their necks and then the actual Chronicles, and the people's reactions at the daily Gathering. And I can envision the disappointed expressions on my parents' faces when, day after day, no report from Eva arrives. But news about Aleksandr and Neils' Relics does.

By late afternoon of the sixth *sinik*, the ice wall becomes sapphire, and I gaze up at the sliver of sky I can see from my perch. I have maybe a bell before the first horn of evening sounds, and the Sun makes Her descent. I hold my *naneq* close to my hollow for the millionth time. It seems that the grey shadow is nearing the surface, but I've thought that many, many times over the past few *siniks*.

Shaking my head to clear it, I examine the ice again. It truly looks darker, as if that damned elusive shadow is finally surfacing from the ice.

I grab my pick and scrape at the emerging shape. After a few ticks, my pick meets with a resistance different than ice or snow. I hitch my *naneq* to a Claim stake and use my trowel along with the pick. My heart pounds. I can see it! The object is oblong and about the size of my pack. But I can't get a clear fix on it just yet. A stubborn layer of ice clings to the artifact like winter frost, and I strip it away as hastily as I dare.

This . . . *thing* materializes in the low light of my *naneq*. It glows like a rare jewel in the white-blue of the crevasse wall. The color is unlike anything I've ever seen before. In the Aerie, the closest shade would be found in the Ark— in the radishes that grow underground in the autumn, or the rare raspberries that burst forth from their delicate bushes in the summer. Or sometimes, you might see something like it in the long sunsets.

What is the name of that color again? I think Lukas used it once for me.

Oh, yeah: pink.

XXV

Aprilus 16
Year 242, A.H.

"Relic!" I call out. My breathless voice echoes loudly throughout the crevasse—too loudly, really—but I don't care. It's finally my turn.

The Climber takes tick after tick to reach me, and the wait feels unendurable, particularly in the fading sunlight. My pick and trowel are at the ready, and I'm dying to pry that pink treasure out of its ice grave. Just when I think I cannot wait another tick, the Climber scuttles down the ice wall. It's the Climber from my first *sinik* in the crevasse, the one with the shock of white hair. I feel uncomfortable under his steady gaze as we start the ritualistic exchange.

"Are you ready to remove the Relic from the ice, Testor?" he asks.

I feel like screaming "yes." Instead, I answer calmly in

the sacred response, "Yes. It nears the surface, but hasn't hit the air."

"I have the Relic bag ready. You may begin, Testor."

I start chipping out the artifact. I'm so eager to remove the stubborn last layer of ice that I wield my pick a little too roughly. "With care, Eva. With care," the Climber whispers.

His gentle advice and his use of my name startle me, and I turn away from my Claim to look at him. The Climber meets my eyes. His unflinching gaze makes me feel embarrassed by my reaction. Why do his words surprise me? Is it the advice, or is it that he called me Eva? Both would be frowned upon by the Triad, no doubt. As a Climber, he would be briefed on all the Testors—their names, their family backgrounds, their skills—so, of course, he would know my Water-name. Is it that he's a Boundary person? A Boundary person wouldn't ordinarily address a Maiden of the Aerie so familiarly, although I never minded when Lukas called me Eva. Then again, I had to beg him. I don't know why I feel so funny around this Climber.

I return to my Claim and work a little slower. Soon the Relic reveals itself. The pink material covering the object doesn't feel like any animal skin or weave spun in the Aerie that I've ever seen. It has a consistent pattern and texture that is somehow smooth yet bumpy, all at once. What animal could have yielded this skin? No, it's not animal hide. The pre-Healing people made fabrics out of all sorts of unnatural materials and by unnatural means.

I chisel around its oblong perimeter. Locked in place for the past two hundred and fifty years, the object releases with a whoosh that sends me flying. I swing back and forth over the crevasse with the Relic gripped in my hands. I know I should reach out to stop myself from getting lanced by one of the jagged ice formations jutting from the opposing wall, but I won't risk dropping my Relic.

Without a word, the Climber pulls me back to my Claim. My heart thumps again. This is forbidden. Why has he helped me once again? Did Jasper put him up to it? Did my parents? I cannot imagine any one of them breaking The Lex so egregiously to protect me in the Testing, no matter how much they care about me.

I nod my thanks to this Boundary person, who of course does not respond. As if nothing unusual had happened between us, he motions for me to slide my Relic into the special bag he hands me. We are suddenly performing the rituals again as proscribed in The Lex. I place the Relic carefully into the bag. Then I take the bag back from the Climber and put it into my pack.

I say a special thanks to the Gods and start my ascent. With the Climber at my back, subtly pushing me along, I make it to the top with a couple of ticks to spare. I'm desperate to tear open the Relic bag and discover just what I've found, but I have to comply with the rituals or lose my Claim. As soon as we reach *terra firma*, the Climber leaves me to report my Relic discovery to the Scouts, who, in turn, are supposed record it into the Testing book.

I don't trust that Scout Okpik will allow the recording to transpire without some kind of protest. So I wait, watching the ritual in its entirety. Okpik listens intently as the Climber describes my Relic.

"Pink?" I hear him say loudly across the Testing Site.

Okpik scoffs and glances over at me with a little smirk, and then enters my find into the book without a fight. I guess he thinks my find is worthless—especially after Aleksandr and Neils's discovery.

I don't care. I have a chance. Maybe not at winning the Archon Laurels, but at surviving—which is the key out here. I have my Relic. I clutch the bag to me, tight as I dare. I must wait until I return to my igloo to examine it—and even then, under the watchful eyes of a Scout-Reliquon—so I look around the Testing Site. The other Testors are clambering to the surface.

The final horn of the evening sounds. I look around to see if anyone notices the Relic in my hands. No one glances my way except Jasper, who gives me a little grin. I know he's watched how the days without a discovery have weighed upon me; I've caught him staring at me. The more I've observed him in return, the less I suspect him of hidden motives. I believe that he really was looking out for me in the crevasse on that first *sinik*, simply as a Gallant. I think that he might have even finagled access to a secret map, maybe that of his grandfather Magnus, so he would be sure to stay ahead of me in the Testing. To keep an eye on me. Not to win. Or maybe to do both. Which, in a way, I love.

I sneak a smile back at him.

The communal meal over the fire passes by in a blur of hurried eating and rushed prayers to the Gods. I just want to get to the solitude of my igloo. But then the moment arrives. When it's just me and my Relic and a hefty Scout-Reliquon—one I don't know—invading the tiny space of my igloo, I feel scared. What if I handle the object improperly? Some Relics are so delicate they can fall apart once their icy coffin melts around them. Every year, after coming so far, at least one Testor loses for that reason. I did not want to be that Testor this year. Mentally, I review Eamon's notes on the safe thawing of artifacts.

No matter how eager, always act slowly; the Relic is fragile and could disintegrate at an overly hasty touch. Light your work space, but be certain to keep the warmth of the flame at a distance. Warm the air steadily, and remember that it might take more than one evening to thaw the Relic safely. Only if you must—if the Relic is refusing to emerge—use the smallest of picks to gently scrape and loosen the ice around the Relic and then return to the process of warming the air around the Relic with patience.

On the sealskin mat work area I've set up in my igloo, I set up two lighted *naneqs*. Mindful of the Scout-Reliquon's stare, I retrieve the supply of caribou moss that I collected in the Taiga. The Scout-Reliquon smiles, I think. Perhaps he knows what I've learned about the prevention of decay from my time in the Ark. I wonder what else he knows. I slide the pink object out of the bag. Its vivid color looks startling—even kind of riotous—here in the center of the black mat in the all-white igloo. I close my eyes for a brief tick, trying to imagine a world where such bright, unnatural colors were commonplace. A world where everything wasn't the Lex-sanctified white or grey or black. Or Gods-given ice-blue or blood-red or animal-brown. This is New North. I simply cannot picture anything else.

The exterior of the Relic has thawed. It is roughly the size of my pack, and a bit lighter. Turning it over, I see that the object—which is unadorned on the front—has two wide pieces of identical cloth attached to its back in an arc. I cannot think of a possible purpose for these odd strips of material. I haven't seen anything like it in any of Eamon's carefully transcribed histories of the Testings.

Careful not to put too much pressure on the material, I turn the Relic this way and that. The more I examine it, the more I think the pieces of cloth look like the straps of my pack. I don't want to stretch the material to the point of tearing, so I align it with my back to see if the straps would fit. They do.

So it is a pack of some sort. Does that mean the Relic holds something else inside? Something even more important than the pink object itself?

My heart starts up again. If it's true that the Relic is a case or pack, how in the Gods do I open it? I don't see an opening on any side. One edge of the Relic is lined with a metallic edge that, upon closer examination, looks a little bit like clenched teeth. I assume it's decorative—as so many things were in the days before the Healing—but then I play with the metal tab at the end of the edging.

I stop breathing. The Relic opens with a strange "z" sort of sound.

Four objects spill out onto the sealskin mat. Each item is encased by a clear coating I assume is a thin layer of ice. What else would so tightly cover an object and yet be so transparent? Yet, when I look at each item—careful not to touch and unduly warm the delicate artifacts—I realize I am wrong. The objects are enclosed by translucent pouches.

Incredible. What are these strange transparent sacs made of? And, more importantly, how can I get the objects out of them? There's nothing in Eamon's journal addressing such things, and I've never heard past Testors mention them. But I have read that pre-Healing materials sometimes melt when they got too close to flame or warmth. I'd hate to destroy this cache so carelessly. Eyes wide, I examine the items without touching them or bringing my *naneq* too close. I notice the Scout-Reliquon holds his breath, too.

Getting as near as I dare, I study one pouch that contains

a rectangular black object, decorated by a triangle with the word *Prada*. What is a "Prada"? I've never heard that word in English, Latin, Boundary, or the odd smattering of French, Finnish, Swedish, and Russian—the pre-Healing languages that work their way into everyday talk in the Aerie. Prada doesn't sound like any of the false charms and talismans associated with Apple or his demons. It isn't one of the names that come up in The Lex or in one of the prayers we recite in the Basilika. And, just by looking at the black triangle, I can't figure out what a Prada is supposed to be.

My pulse quickens. This is a true discovery. Unprecedented. My curiosity gets to me, and against the better judgment of probably every Archon and Testor in New North, I seize the pouch. The Scout-Reliquon gasps, but I'm so fixated on this Prada that I barely hear him. I expect the object to be hard, but its translucent material is flexible, like the woven cloth we use to make our gowns in the Aerie. In fact, it's so unexpectedly wiggly that I drop it.

The pouch hits the sealskin mat and splits open. Many small rectangles spill out of the Prada into the clear sack. The rectangles have colorful stripes and patterns on them, and I kneel close. All are emblazoned with strange words: Visa, American Express, Nordea Bank Finland, and Kirov Ballet. But only one is instantly recognizable: MasterCard, the wicked currency promoted by Apple and his demons. I shudder involuntarily at being so close to an evil thing. The mirror has been in my home since I was born; I've always known it. But this is different. Being so close to an evil thing that hasn't been sanctified by ritual scares me. And perhaps these other rectangles are MasterCard's minions.

A simple white rectangle pokes out from the pile. In all this color and design, its plainness draws me in. I take a closer look. A minuscule image of a girl is somehow grafted onto its surface. The likeness is so startlingly real that I jump back, bumping into the Scout-Reliquon. Chiding myself for being ridiculous, I mutter an apology and bend back toward the image. I smooth out a ripple in the translucent pouch to get a better look at the girl's face. With her fair hair and bright blue eyes, the girl in the picture is beautiful. If you ignore all the paint on her face, of course. And she appears to be about my age.

How did the pre-Healing people make such a lifelike picture? I've never seen anything like it in the Aerie. Pigments are so rare. Even those sacred tapestries woven out of dyed thread for the Basilica or for diptychs look rudimentary compared with this. Only then do I notice tiny writing underneath the picture. The word *nimi* is there; I recognize the Finnish word for name from the Finnish-origin Founding families who occasionally still use the word. Beneath *nimi* are two words: Elizabet Laine. And then I know. The girl in the picture—the girl to whom the Prada and all of these artifacts belonged—was called Elizabet Laine.

XXVI

Aprilus 16
Year 242, A.H.

Elizabet Laine. Those two words make the owner of my Relics come alive, something I didn't expect. I don't recall a single Testor ever mentioning the owner of their Relics. Maybe they didn't find anything linking their artifacts to a particular person, or maybe they thought the artifact itself was more instructive than the person who once owned, used, or even loved the Relic they found. But I cannot ignore the presence of Elizabet Laine in these Relics. She is everywhere.

Ignoring the Scout-Reliquon's glare, I lean within inches of the four translucent pouches. I know I am taking risks by handling the items and rushing a little, but I don't care. I must know this Elizabet Laine.

"Caution," the Scout-Reliquon whispers. He's not supposed

to offer judgment or guidance, only protect the Relics with that single word while the Testors work. Taking a risk, I ignore him. Again.

The second sack contains a smaller open bag patterned in vivid stripes of yellow and pink. I gently shake it, and the smaller bags contents pour out: small tubes and vials and bottles. I notice two brownish-colored bottles have lettering on them—*for depression*—and a third says *for pain*. I've heard of these pre-Healing diseases before, sicknesses of the soul, but don't know much about them. I'll look for those terms in my pre-Healing Histories later, when the Scout-Reliquon takes the Relics away for the night for safekeeping. Then I see the word *Prozac* on one of the bottles. Instinctively, I drop the sack, horrified. I know that word. Prozac is one of Apple's most prized and wicked remedies.

Placing the sack down on the mat, I turn my attention to the third pouch. The objects within seem much more recognizable at first. I spot a knife not unlike my *ulu*, and something that resembles my water pouch, though of an odd material. I see a piece of metal and a rock-like material similar to the objects we use to make fire, as well as a few candles. I catch a glimpse of a circular object with a dial and arrow, kind of like the lodestones we use to tell direction. One item is especially strange to me: a black oblong tube with no purpose I can discern. But otherwise, the items resemble those I might pack to go hunting or out into the wilderness.

I reach for the fourth sack, which holds just one rectangular object. It looks pretty bland at first, until I get really close. Then, I see the words *Kirov Ballet* inscribed in gold on the cover, and next to it, a tiny lifelike picture of a dancer dressed in teensy scraps of clothing. The girl is nearly naked.

It's my turn to gasp out loud, and when I do, the Scout-Reliquon rushes to my side. He holds his lamp dangerously near the fourth sack. Before I can make a single move, he carefully lifts up the pink pack and the translucent pouches and slips them into the Relic bag. "I think we've had quite enough excitement for today, Testor. You will be permitted to study your Relics again after the dig tomorrow evening."

And then he leaves my igloo. Leaving me alone with endless questions. Because the nearly naked dancer in that tiny, lifelike picture is Elizabet Laine.

XXVII

Aprilus 18, 19, 20, 21, 22, and 23
Year 242, A.H.

ll I want to do is stay in the igloo, making sense of Elizabet Laine's belongings and of her strange pre-Healing life. Her Chronicle is starting to form in my mind, and I'm eager to begin it. Especially since I think this discovery might actually give me a chance at the Archon Laurels. It is so unlike anything I'd imagined finding.

But I can't begin. Not yet anyway. The spring thaw hasn't started, so all us Testors must continue with our Claim digs until the Site is closed down as unsafe. The Triad—and all the people waiting back in the Aerie—want us to find more and more. I'll do my duty. But what could I possibly unlock from the ice that would be more compelling than Elizabet Laine's pack?

My fellow Testors seem eager to descend into the

crevasse each of those six mornings. Even Aleksandr and Neils. When that horn sounds out, they race to the Site ready to begin, as if it is the first day of the dig. Why? Aleksandr and Neils have already found key Relics. From overheard whispers in the crevasse, I know that the other Testors have all uncovered Relics of educational value. Jacques found a box of remedies—including Tylenols— which will cause an even greater furor in the Aerie town square than Prozacs. Benedict, Petr, and Thurstan all found cartons containing silver-foiled packets of foodstuffs that look nothing like food. William discovered the metallic nets of a fishing boat, and Jasper unearthed the machine designed to make that boat travel quickly through the seas. The pre-Healing people hated fish and water. I couldn't hear what Knud located—maybe he hasn't found any- thing, he seems so lackluster since the news about Tristan.

Any of these Relics would garner a Testor a solid chance at winning the Archon Laurels. Only an artifact that served in direct tribute to the false god Apple would beat them out. And such a treasure hasn't been found for nearly one hun- dred and fifty years. Not since Madeline.

Yet, even though they all scamper back to their igloos at night, not a single one of the Testors has begun to send Chronicles back to the Aerie by carrier pigeon. Surely their Relics bear cautionary tales worthy of a Chronicle, and the first to send in a Chronicle always seems to gain an edge. Oddly, they all seem determined to find something else, something rarer and more interesting.

Are they trying to top my discovery?

There's no way they could have learned about my find. Only the pink pack was registered in the Testing book; I have not instructed the Scout-Reliquon to enter the pack's contents yet. I want to make better sense of the items first. And there's no way the other Testors could have access to my Relics during the day; all the Relics are under the Scout-Reliquons' guard. Unless Scout Okpik is conspiring with my assigned Scout-Reliquon and others against me? But I can't give into my suspicions.

I don't want the other Testors sniffing around my Claim, and I still don't trust Aleksandr and Neils even though they haven't done anything untoward. Yet. So I pretend I'm still looking for a worthy Relic. I arrive at the lineup for the first horn of morning as if I'd rested the night before instead of furiously studying Elizabet's belongings during the short time allotted me by the Scout-Reliquon. I belay down the crevasse wall as if I am desperate to locate a teaching artifact. I dig into the wall and siphon off rivers of water as if I must make my Claim yield. And I give Jasper pitiable half-smiles when he looks down to see how I'm faring. I need him to believe in the paucity of my findings too, although I feel a little guilty about deceiving him.

As I go through the motions of the excavation, I dream of Elizabet's belongings and what I've learned about them during the past six evenings. I think about the first pouch, with the Prada and the multi-colored rectangles that fit within its little slots. I believe that they are some form of currency—like Euros—which the pre-Healing people had to earn and use to pay for life's necessities; I'm pretty sure that's true of the MasterCard anyway. Incredibly, pre-Healing leaders didn't think it was their job to dispense food or provide a safe home for their people. The leaders assigned false values to this currency and forced their people to barter for survival with worthless MasterCards. The Keeper of the Ark wouldn't dream of denying anyone the fruits of the harvest. *Pari passu*, the Keeper always says at Harvest time, quoting The Lex, of course. And all the Triad members echo that view, in words and actions

I think about Elizabet using the patterned bag within the second clear sack. It turns out that the colorful vials and bottles are Maybellines and Chanels—kinds of face paint— a sad statement about the pre-Healing values and the sin of Vanity. The three brown bottles—including the Prozac—are remedies for mysterious pre-Healing diseases called pain and depression. I know what pain is, of course. And I know that depression is a kind of pain of the mind. But I think it is odd that they suffered so much, considering that they didn't know the Healing was coming, that their deaths were near. Maybe they somehow knew that their lives were empty and false? And anyway, the Founders told us that these conditions had no magical cure.

THE NIGHT OF THE sixth *sinik*, I discover what I must do.

It stems from the moment I touch a small button on the mysterious oblong black object I found in the third sack. A bright, bluish light shoots out from it. A light that reminds me of the one that shone on my tent the night Scout Okpik visited me. It's hard to imagine a world where light came at the mere touch of a finger, instead of arduous ticks with flint and steel over hard-won wood. The pre-Healing people lived in a world of luxury and indulgence, and had no appreciation for it. As for the knife, lodestone, and water sack, well, I still can't figure out why a girl living in a bustling pre-Healing city would have need for them. They are items used for hunting. All I can figure is that they were sentimental trinkets of a past time before the world became so full and crazy.

Before it vanishes, the light strikes the "Kirov Ballet" book I've discovered in the last clear pouch, which contains countless lifelike renderings of dancers in practically no clothing, in all sorts of lewd poses. They have the same precise, realistic appearance as the image on the card with the word *nimi*. And the dancer who appears in most of the pictures is Elizabet Laine.

Yet the images that move me most are the sketches in a greyish ink along the page borders, the ones that bear a more homemade look. Pictures that seem as though Elizabet had drawn them herself, especially since they bear her initials. Here, a lone dancer is shown on stage in series of uncomfortable contortions before a sea of leering faces. Again, the barely clothed dancer closely resembles Elizabet.

Elizabet looks so exposed. And so very, very cold.

Poor, poor Elizabet. I wish I could cover up her shame. From the humiliation of exposing her body nightly and her spirit daily, with none of the Maidenly protections that the Aerie affords young women. She had none of the Lex-sanctified rules that I benefit from every day, even if I bristle at them from time to time. Maybe my mother has some justification for all her Lex adherence after all.

Because of this, I almost don't want to share my Relics with anyone, even though there is no precedent for this discovery. Eamon's meticulous research into past Testings has shown me that. Not even the stuff of rumors. My discovery could be unusual—even legendary. Like my father's mirror.

But I believe that it's much more.

I don't know why. Maybe it's Eamon's death. Maybe it's Lukas's map. Maybe it's the conspiracy against me

thrilling
Mariinsky
ends and
ents as the

Irina Kostova and Elizabet Laine in Giselle.

ny
Our
ncers
e your
chnical
dramatic
h beloved
wan Lake,
Sylvia

that I detect in whispers and glances. But I feel like this is a Gods-given sign. Elizabet Laine sent me this gift from the days before the Healing. With this offering comes a Gods-entrusted duty to Elizabet and to the people of New North— to the past and to the present. I must write a new sort of Chronicle, not simply a cautionary tale of how an object led to the world's downfall and necessitated the cleansing waters of the Healing.

How will I do this? I have never heard—or read—a Chronicle that wasn't simply a story of a Relic and the horrific damage it inflicted.

Then it comes to me. My Chronicle will not be just the story of Elizabet's pink pack and its contents, but the story of Elizabet. I will tell the story of a life lost in the end . . . lost even before the Healing. And I will tell Elizabet's story as if I was seeing those final days through Elizabet's eyes. As if I was her, one of the many sinners who brought about the Healing.

My heart races at the thought of writing this unusual Chronicle. My mother and father will approve; Lukas will approve; Jasper will approve . . . Eamon would have approved. And this is how I will win. This is how a Maiden can become an Archon.

The Chronicle of Elizabet Laine, Part I

I am lost. Horribly lost. I thought I'd made the proper turn when I left the doctor's office, but the St. Petersburg streets are a dense warren of dead ends and intersecting roadways. The buildings are starting to look familiar, and I'm pretty sure I've made a circle.

The panic starts to build inside me. I'm going to be late. Very late. What will the Keeper of the Ballet do to me?

It doesn't help my fear that the streets are melting as I go further and further into the warren. The sky-touching buildings grow less and less ornate; instead, they look more like decaying stone towers about to topple onto the garbage heaps lining the streets. I can't believe people actually live in these teetering steeples stacked one upon another like a deck of cards, but the fresh piles of discarded Cokes and Hersheys on the balconies speak to their habitation. These are the homes of the Penny class. They aren't even afforded the decoration of the metal trees that line the central St. Petersburg streets where the Euro class lives. It's beyond bleak in here.

Although it's still afternoon, the skies are growing dark from the black clouds emitting from the factories. No Electrics light the backstreets, save for the Neons of the adverts for Cokes and Maybellines and, of course, the God Apple. In this darkness, I'm finding it increasingly hard to sidestep the rubbish . . . and the people.

In some ways, the people are familiar enough. Like most in St. Petersburg, the males wear tight-fitting Levis and tops with stripes and bright patterns, and the females wear Minis and Manolos—just like me. As with many in St. Petersburg, the males leer at the females, and the females competitively scan each other's costumes. And just like those on the Euro streets, they hold close to their faces the little worship tablets to the God Apple, so they can whisper prayers, something I find myself doing more and more these days. Although these people are probably praying for more Pennies. I pray for help of a different kind.

But these people do look different than those in the Euro parts of St. Petersburg that I normally frequent. Different than me. They are coughing, and they bear the pasty, pale skin of sickness. At any tick, one of their bodies—weakened by the food and the remedies—could spread a Plague, and I want to avoid brushing against them at all costs.

But it isn't easy to remain untouched amidst the garbage and the throngs of people, and my shoe stick catches on a Coke. I tumble to the cracking, stone ground—no grass exists in St. Petersburg to break my fall—and find myself face-to-face with one of the Homeless. His face is caked with grime from the air and streets. The Homeless is Penniless and can't afford food, and he's so thin that his bones nearly poke through the skin. I see this through the holes in the garbage bag he wears for clothes. For a tick, I am mesmerized by the awfulness of his situation and can't move my eyes or body away from him.

The Homeless mistakes my momentary paralysis for injury. Despite his own bodily weakness, the Homeless tries to rise and help me up. I flinch away from his touch—the Homeless are known to spread all sorts of Plagues—and push myself to standing. I check to make sure my pink pack is still on my back. Then I run.

As I dart in and out of people and trash and Fords, I start to cry. The Homeless was only trying to help—even though no one had ever tried to help him. But what choice did I have? Would I have acted any differently in my Finnish homeland, where the odd tree still grows? Where you can still find a patch of green grass? Probably not. Every man for himself, my father always says. That's what God Apple wants. My father quotes the preachers on the Panasonic.

I see a canal bridge in the distance, and I aim for it. Recalling that I crossed one on my way to the doctor's office, I figure it's my best bet out of the awful Penny backstreets. As I near the bridge, the streets look appreciably cleaner, and the buildings looks less like lean-tos. I mouth a silent plea to Apple that I'm getting close to the Teatralnaya ploshchad.

Apple answers my prayer. Only two streets away, I spy the high white dome and pale green walls of the Mariinsky Theater, home to the Kirov Ballet, the building that dominates the Teatralnaya ploshchad. My calling here is a blessing for my family—Euros to send home to Finland for them—but a curse for me. No matter how I really feel about it in the private chambers of my Spirit, because Apple can see even there.

I break into a sprint. It's nearly a bell to curtain time, and the Keeper of the Ballet will be raging at my absence and screaming at the other Dancers about the whereabouts of his Principal. Soon, the theater will fill with the lavishly dressed men and women of the Euro class, and the Ballet cannot begin without me. Elizabet Laine, Prima Ballerina.

Throwing back the golden gates of the theater entrance, I race past the box office and the crystal lobby to the changing area. I dart into my dressing room, where the Dressers await me. Their faces are full of fear; the Keeper has flown through here on wings of fury, I see. The best thing I can do for the Dressers—for all of them, really—is to ready myself for the Ballet quickly.

I stretch out my arms, and the Dressers strip me of my clothes. In a mere tick, I stand before them completely naked. A few months ago, this would have embarrassed me to the core of my Spirit. But no more. It is what my career requires. It is what Apple demands. My body no longer belongs to me.

The Dressers affix to my body flimsy, sheer pieces of fabric. They lace onto my feet silken shoes with hard, wooden toes. They wrap my white-blonde hair into a complicated knot on the top of my head, and weave glistening jewels through it. But they leave my face to me.

I draw close to the mirror. I open my pink pack and pull from it a bag of yellow and pink stripes. As I do, my hand brushes against the packet of gear I used in Finland when I entered the rare smatterings of wilderness still left. Even though it serves no purpose here in Russia, I keep the gear in my pack to remind me of the time before my calling came—when I was still free to breathe forest air.

But I can't allow myself to think about that now. Pulling out my Maybellines and Chanels from the bag, I spread them onto the counter. I begin to paint the face of another person upon my own. After I draw the last stripe of black across my lids and the final swoosh of red on my lips, I look in the mirror. The Elizabet I used to be—the girl romping through the vestiges of the Finnish forest, with wild hair and emerging freckles—is gone. I am replaced by the mask of a Kirov Prima Ballerina.

The dread at my calling begins to pound through me. The endless pivots and turns and bodily contortions that will be expected of me tonight course through my mind. The staring eyes and ogling looks and wild claps from the audience creep into my thoughts. The nightly exposure of self and sacrifice of Spirit—done for the audience's pleasure at Apple's bidding—washes over me.

But then I remember. The remedies.

I reach into my pink pack. Glancing around to make sure no one is watching, I place two remedy pills on my tongue. One for the pain that the Dance inflicts upon my body. And a Prozac for the dark depression that Dance inflicts upon my Spirit.

The Keeper yells for me. Before I answer his call, I take a tick to whisper into my worship tablet. Staring into its blank surface, I beg Apple to send the relief that the doctor promised. Then I step out into the hallway.

The Keeper looks me over, adjusting a feather draping over my right breast and tugging the sheer bodice of my costume down just a little farther. The audience likes this, I know. They like to see my flesh. He nods his approval and spins me in the direction of the stage.

The other Dancers part to let me through to the red curtain. I take my place near the opening in its enormous folds. I peek out at the gleaming gold walls and sparkling lights and filled blue chairs, expecting the nightly terror to settle in. But it doesn't. The remedies begin to work.

The darkness of my Spirit and body lifts, and I become someone else inside and out. I feel no shame, no humiliation. I am not me. I am someone capable of sacrificing herself for Apple.

XXVIII

Aprilus 23
Year 242, A.H.

The Chronicle starts off slowly. But then it courses through me, aided by the forbidden Faerie tales told by my Nurse Aga, and the secret myths shared by Lukas, and the stories I made up myself to entertain Eamon. The Chronicle flows from my fingers as if Elizabet's hand holds my quill and writes the words herself. I become Elizabet.

During the bells of writing, Elizabet and her world grow so real to me that when dawn breaks and I must stop, I blink at my white world of snow and ice as if it has become the dream. And the cacophonic world in the days just before the Healing has become the reality.

But then my dogs begin barking, desperate to be fed. The camp starts to rustle with the sounds of the Boundary servers preparing breakfast, the Testors readying. I am drawn away from the pre-Healing world and back into New North and the Testing.

Before I lose my nerve, I roll my Chronicle as small as I can. I march over to the Bird-Master and hand over the first pages of Elizabet's story. He is not permitted to review what I've written, only to send. As he slides the Chronicle into the container at the carrier pigeon's neck, I hold my breath. I watch the bird soar into the sky—due south—taking a part of me along with him.

Within a bell, I'm back down in the crevasse chipping away at the ice wall as if nothing ever happened. As if I've never stepped back into Elizabet's world. Back into time.

Yet I'm changed. I am altered by this brush-up with a real person who lived and breathed and danced and trembled and loved in the days before the Earth's waters rose up and submerged wickedness in a watery grave. No longer is the Healing just something my parents and Teachers and Basilikons lectured me about, a time and place so long ago that it defies comprehension. It is very real, and it is inhabited by someone I know well.

In some ways, this wisdom makes me reluctant to return to Elizabet's Chronicle. I know what comes next. I don't want to experience those last days of terror. And I think it will be hard for the people of New North to experience them along with me. But I can't help myself; as my body balances in a crevasse of ice, my mind journeys back. When I return to my igloo tonight, I will write.

The Chronicle of Elizabet Laine, Part II

The pirouettes propel me across the stage of the Mariinsky Theater. With the remedies in me, I feel so free of pain that I spin faster than ever before. The audience cheers my performance, awarding me with bouquet after bouquet of flowers and a shower of MasterCards. The remedies have worked their magic.

The remedies take away the shame of so many strangers' staring eyes. The remedies allow me to smile—instead of flinch—while being fawned over at the Patron Gallant party after the ballet. The remedies permit me to tolerate their leers and proprietary caresses.

The Keeper is pleased with my newfound compliance in the days that follow. The better I perform—on stage and at the parties—the more Euros that ballet makes and the more patronage bestowed upon the Kirov. This means more Euros for me, too. Euros that I send to my family in Finland, who desperately need the currency. Their MasterCards have been made worthless. The Rulers can do that to a family and a farm.

I should be happy. I tell myself that I am doing the right thing by dancing. The necessary thing. The very thing that Apple wants from me.

But in the solitude of my room—stacked high with other such rooms in a tower of dizzying heights—the disgrace is hard to bear. If my parents truly understood what I'm doing for those Euros, surely they'd beg me to return home. Surely they wouldn't want the tainted currency, I tell myself.

Or would they? Isn't my father the one who encouraged me toward this calling? Isn't he the one who said Apple wants me to succeed at this career? Didn't my mother nod along as he urged me toward this path? Sending me forth with her silence?

The very thought that my family might take the Euros

no matter the cost to my Spirit makes me feel more alone.
I turn on the Panasonic for distraction. But I am greeted
with far worse than any pain.

Image after image of rising ocean waters appear on
the device. The Media reports that—all over the world—the
coasts are flooding. Ice is melting. The Media urges people
to take heed and seek higher ground.

"No, it can't be true," I whisper to myself.

I feel woozy from the news and the barrage of horrible
images. Kneeling before my Apple diptych, I begin to pray,
"O Apple, who art in Heaven, hallowed be Thy name . . ."

Despite my supplications, the blank diptych offers no
answers. No solace. I feel darkness descend upon my Spirit,
and as if in a dream, I'm drawn to my jars of remedies.
I've been reserving them for performance days only, but
would it really hurt to take one more tonight? Just this
once? I place a Prozac on my tongue, and within a few
ticks, I feel a relief that Apple alone used to provide.

XXIX
Aprilus 24
Year 242, A.H.

I am again imagining Elizabet's last days when I hear the cry of "Relic." It jolts me out of my daydreaming. I'd guessed that this crevasse was tapped out, something that often happens when the Test days are winding down. I'd guessed wrong.

"Relic," I hear again, and I realize that it's coming from right overhead. From Jasper. His voice is excited, and I stop my ruse of chiseling into the ice wall to listen. Even when he discovered his boat machine—an engine, I think I heard it called—he didn't sound like this. What in the Gods has he found?

Digging as quietly as I can, I wait for the Boundary Climber to make his way to Jasper. I hear the Climber belay down, and I pray to the Gods that the crevasse structure will let me hear even a whisper of their conversation. Unlike the last Relic Jasper found, which I had to learn about from stray comments between Scouts.

"Are you ready to remove the Relic from the ice, Testor?" the Climber asks in the ritualistic way.

"Yes. It nears the surface, but hasn't hit the air," Jasper responds, also in the ceremonial fashion.

"I have the Relic bag ready. You may begin, Testor."

Scrapes fill the air, and within a tick, I hear the familiar whoosh of the Relic removed from its grave of ice. Less familiar is the sound of the Climber letting out a little gasp.

"It has the sign of Apple on it!" The Climber sounds astonished; he's lost the slow cadence of the ritualistic exchange.

"I know. Can you believe it?" Jasper answers, his voice giddy.

I freeze. *The Apple symbol.* Has Jasper just won the second and third set of Advantages? Have I lost the Laurels before they even come close to my head?

Tears well up in my eyes.

The Chronicle of Elizabet deserves to win. If the people of New North, and the Triad along with them, really listen to the story in Elizabet's Relics, they will learn something far more important than the tired old tale that an Apple Relic will tell.

I hope I'm not just being petty and greedy. I know I should be happy for Jasper for making such a significant find, especially if our parents' plans work out and we end up Betrothed. But I want to win; I don't just want to be married to the Chief Archon like my mother. Even if we don't end up in a Union, maybe I could strike a deal with Jasper, kind of like the rumors of past alliances, indeed the rumors that swirl around his uncle and my father. It would be fitting in a way. Yet, what would I ask for in exchange for my support of him? The only thing I really want is the Archon Laurels.

Only a bell or so until the final horn of evening, but still I go through the motions of pretending to work the crevasse wall. Even if I found something, nobody would care, not with the news of Jasper's amazing discovery. Not even Aleksandr or Neils, if they ever had any interest in me at all, that is. As I scrape away at the stubborn ice wall, my mind drifts back to Elizabet's Chronicle.

I know that I'll return to my quill and paper when the *sinik* is over. Elizabet deserves to have her last ticks memorialized instead of being lost in the waters of the Healing. I almost feel I owe it to Elizabet to write the best Chronicle I possibly can. Is it Eamon's death that propels me, too? Does it even matter? I will finish. And then I'll send my Chronicles back to the Aerie and leave the decision to the Gods.

The Chronicle of Elizabet Laine, Part III

I stand on the stage of the Mariinsky Theater, ready for the orchestra to commence. All the Kirov Dancers are supposed to be practicing for the Ballet's debut of La Bayadere, and the stage should be filled. But I am alone. The Panasonic reports have driven them all away. For hours Media has been advising people to evacuate the port city. One by one, the Corps Dancers left the stage, as their family members arrived at the theater in tears. Then the Principals decamped as loved ones stood at the stage door, begging for them to leave. But no one comes for me—my family is far away in Finland—so I stay. Where else would I go?

Anyway, even though I've been offering prayers to Apple

just in case, I can't fully believe the broadcasts. It doesn't seem possible that the ancient streets of St. Petersburg could be submerged as Media threatens. The city has withstood so many ravages over the centuries, why would it fall now? And truly, would the Keeper really continue the Ballet if the world was about to end?

The remaining violinist begins to play, and I ready my body for the grueling opening of La Bayadere. Just as I'm about to extend my arms and legs for the arabesque, the Keeper yells out, "Elizabet! Come backstage!"

I lower my legs and arms and race to the back. What have I done wrong? The Keeper never interferes with the final rehearsal unless my dancing is absolutely horrific. And I've barely begun.

The Keeper is waiting just behind the red curtain's final fold. "Gather your things. There is a Patron who will take you to safe passage on his boat. And me along with you."

"A Patron?" What in the name of Apple is the Keeper talking about?

"Yes." The Keeper whispers the Patron's Water-name.

I recognize it. He is one of my most ardent admirers, one who sends flowers to the stage every evening and who sits alone in a special box seat leering at me night after night. One whose caresses grow more and more proprietary with every Patron party. He is rumored to be among the richest men in St. Petersburg. And the most corrupt. The very thought of him makes me shiver. Out of fear.

Still, the Keeper's command confuses me. "You mean, he'll take us tonight? After the performance?"

"No, Elizabet. We must go right now." For the first time since I've known him, the Keeper looks scared.

His expression immobilizes me. If the Keeper—a powerful

official who terrifies so many—is actually scared, could Media's reports be true? Media is a liar: sometimes on Apple's side, sometimes not.

"Now, Elizabet! This may be our only chance," the Keeper screams at me, shaking me out of my reverie.

I run back to my dressing room. Stripping off my practice clothes, I search around for something suitable to wear on a boat. My Mini and Manolos won't do. I poke my head into one of the other dancer's cubicles and grab the Levis and boots left behind by one of the male dancers in his haste to leave. Pulling on his clothes, I reach for my pink pack.

The very tick I step out of my dressing room, the Keeper grabs my hand. "We must run."

There is no need to duck and weave through the corridors of the Mariinsky Theater. The normally teeming hallways are deserted, and we make their way to the gilded front doors in record time. When we push the heavy doors open, I don't recognize the streets outside.

The Teatralnaya ploshchad—usually so orderly and elegant—is falling apart. The streets are slick with water. Thousands of people—Euro, Penny, and Homeless in one enormous mass—crush the streets. They carry babies in their arms and overstuffed packs on their backs, and they are trying to run.

Then I discover why. I can hear the sound of rushing water like an underbelly roar beneath the noises the mob makes in trying to flee. The Teatralnaya ploshchad empties into the port on the River Neva and from there into the Bay of Finland on the Baltic Sea. Since these people don't have time to make it inland, they want to ride the rising waters on boats.

The horde is merciless. People have been trampled

underfoot, but I can't let myself to look upon them. I cannot weaken or I'll be down there with them. The Keeper clings to my hand like a life preserver, because that it is exactly what I am for him. Without me, I realize, he has no ticket on the Patron's boat.

"Where are the Guards?" I yell to the Keeper over the sound of the throngs.

"They were among the first to evacuate. Don't forget, they control the boats." He yells back.

The people of St. Petersburg have been abandoned. The Guards, the men sworn to protect us from within and without, have deserted us. The citizens of St. Petersburg must face this catastrophe alone.

In the distance, I hear screaming. I realize that the sound comes from the direction of the port, and within a few ticks, a wave of water rushes down the street. Bodies and debris rain down with it, bringing death closer to me by the tick. The screaming now comes from my own throat. Drenched and disoriented, I clutch onto the Keeper's hand. I need him as much as he needs me right now. He hasn't told me exactly where the Patron's boat is docked. Intentionally, I'm sure.

To my own surprise, I take charge of the situation. Dragging the Keeper, I sprint the remaining stretch to the port, weaving in and out of the mass of humanity in a frantic dance. Finally we reach the port.

People are hysterical to get closer to the few boats still moored. They leave the weak and old in their wake. I can't bear to look back at the trampled corpses behind them. What is happening to everybody? To me?

"There! His boat is just there!" I hear the Keeper yell over the din.

The Patron's boat—a vast, luxurious vessel—is one of the last left in the port. He waited until the last possible tick for me. As the Keeper and I approach, armed men block our way with raised spears and knives and guns.

The Keeper lifts his hand in a gesture of peace and calls out. "I am the Keeper of the Kirov Ballet. And I have brought Elizabet Laine as the Patron requested."

He pushes me toward them as his offering. The men lower their weapons and reach out for my hand. They pass me to the Patron, this greedy man fat with Euros who has emerged. As soon as I'm safe in the Patron's grasp, the armed men push the Keeper back, away from the dock.

When he fights back, the men throw the Keeper into the rising waters of the River Neva.

As I scream out in horror, the Patron tries to offer me strange comfort. "Sorry, my dear. I only have room for one more."

XXX

Aprilus 25
Year 242, A.H.

I watch the carrier pigeon fly south. The bird carries the final pages of the Chronicle of Elizabet Laine. I'm pretty sure that its message will not win me the Archon Laurels, not given Jasper's find. But I feel strangely satisfied, as if I've truly done my duty by Elizabet and Eamon.

I feel anxious, too. No one was ever written a Chronicle like mine before.

Until now I'd been so wrapped up in writing and winning, I hadn't really thought through other possible repercussions. Will I be accused of Lex-breaking for writing something from a voice that isn't my own? I can't think of a particular Lex rule addressing my Chronicle format, other than the Prohibition of Fictions, but while I know my writing to be the truth, it is wildly different. And, The Lex says the Chronicle must show how the Relic led to mankind's fall or *suffer a punishment worthy of the offense.* I'd been looking forward to finishing up the Testing and heading home—and seeing my father and Lukas and even my mother—but now I feel wary.

Jasper's win should make things easier for me if there is a backlash. After all, my father just wants me to return home alive. Lukas won't be too disappointed that I didn't always follow his advice. I try to repress my worries and focus on the comforts that await.

The mood in the camp is lighter, and not just for me. All the Testors have sent their Chronicles back. The Testing Site will remain open for only this last *sinik.* Spring is coming fast, and the warming brings instability to the ice crevasse. So no more climbing and digging. We're all happy to be going home. All except for Tristan and Anders, of course, and I'm guessing we all try hard not to think about them.

I spend the morning and afternoon bells of our last *sinik* packing up and preparing my dogs for the journey. We linger over dinner instead of racing back to igloos like we've done for so many *siniks.* Technically, The Lex still prohibits talking among Testors, but tonight the Scouts have turned a blind eye to quiet chatter. I guess they figure there's not much collusion we can spawn or advantages we can give each other now. Even still, no one has really bothered to talk to me, so I just sit back and listen to the boys' banter. So far, it consists of a lot of bragging and very little else—but it entertains after so much silence.

Only Jasper is as quiet as I am. Until he pretends to head back to his igloo and whispers as he passes: "Meet me at the crevasse after dinner?"

For a tick, I wonder whether I should risk The Lex to meet

him. But I want to know where we stand before we head home and he is lost in the victory celebrations and Chief Archon preparations. I try to tell myself that I'm happy he'll be taking my father's place at the end of his term. He is the next best thing to Eamon in my family's eyes. Perhaps even in mine. I nod, and after a respectable numbers of ticks, I get up and start walking in the direction of the Testing Site. Casually, I think.

"Testor, where are you going?" one of the Scouts calls out to me.

Why did I think anyone would let me slink off? Even now? "To clear out my gear from the Testing Site, sir."

The Scout pauses, probably figuring there's not much more damage I can do at this stage. Except to myself, which Scout Okpik and possibly some others wouldn't mind. Mercifully, Okpik's been ignoring me for the past few *siniks*. Since Aleksandr and Neils' find, really. "Shouldn't you have done that earlier?"

"Yes, sir."

He sighs. "All right. Just be back before last light."

"Yes, sir."

The light is still bright enough to make the landscape blue and purple instead of unnavigable black, and I make it to the crevasse easily enough. Two Boundary Climbers still patrol the perimeter—to protect the Site from the Testors, or the Testors from the Site, I'm not sure which. The white-haired Climber is one of the two on duty, and I busy myself with collecting gear so I won't have to look him in the eye.

In a quarter bell, Jasper arrives. Kneeling down nearby, he makes a show of packing up his dig equipment as well. I don't want to say the wrong thing, so I let him speak first.

"Feels like we've been beyond the Ring a long time, doesn't it?" he whispers, keeping his eyes fixed on his Claim.

"The Aerie almost seems like a dream," I whisper back. I don't tell him how changed I feel. How Elizabet has altered me in ways I could have never imagined. How sitting here next to Jasper—a genderless Testor with an unsure future instead of a Lex-guarded Maiden—I feel as exposed as Elizabet must have felt onstage. As naked as I might feel on my wedding eve. And how Elizabet has made me as eager to win the Archon Laurels as any Gallant entering the Testing, so much so that I wrote a Chronicle as if I were Elizabet herself.

He moves closer to me. The air grows warmer around us. When he starts talking, I can sense his breath on me. It makes me feel funny, and I almost can't concentrate on his words.

"Things are going to be different when we get back, Eva. They might get really busy for me." He hesitates, as if he shouldn't say what comes next, "You know that I found a small worship tablet to the false god Apple."

"I know," I whisper back.

He laughs a little. "I guess there aren't any secrets out here. Anyway . . . in case I get swept up in all the ceremony, I wanted you to know that my feelings for you haven't changed. If anything, they've gotten deeper. Watching you risk so much out here has given me . . ."

As Jasper speaks, it strikes me that his speech sounds rehearsed instead of heartfelt. My warm feelings start to dissipate. Instead I find myself angry at his assumptions that he's already won—even though I've assumed as much myself—and that I'm nothing more than a Maiden who can be appeased with a bit of Gallant-speak. Maybe he needs a lesson. Or better yet, a bargain: my support of his Archon victory in exchange for a spot as Lexor, just like my father and his uncle were rumored to have made. Why not? I know The Lex inside and out and it would appease me to be the only female in the Triad. It would be even better if Jasper and I do end up Betrothed.

I take a deep breath, but hesitate when one of the Climbers passes close by in his rounds.

Jasper stops talking and begins packing up his ice screws and skeins of sealskin ropes. Just to look busy, I coil a rope, too. Even though it's not mine.

The Climber draws nearer to us. "I understand that your Chronicle is very popular," he remarks.

Both Jasper and I look up; it's the white-haired Climber. Jasper puffs up a little, and says, "Well, it's been a long time since an Apple Relic has been found."

"I wasn't talking to you, Testor. I was talking to her."

"Me?" I ask, incredulous. I'd been praying to the Gods for a positive reaction from New North, but I'm surprised when I hear that I've received it. How could the Aerie populace be favoring my Chronicle? Over Jasper's Apple find? Especially when my Chronicle breaks form?

"Yes." The Climber smiles a little, his teeth white in the mounting darkness. "Some say it's the most popular Chronicle ever." Then he walks away.

Jasper slumps back into the snow. His lips twitch. He is seething, I can tell. "What did you find, Eva?" he asks without even looking at me.

I tell him about the pink pack, all its little marvels. I describe to him my connection to their owner. And I tell him the Chronicle I wrote of Elizabet's life and her last days. I think he'll understand.

"So your Chronicle is a story?"

"Not exactly—"

"Kind of like the fiction they used to write in pre-Healing days?"

He's trying to hurt me. I know better than anyone that "fiction" is a dirty word in the Aerie. Outlawed by The Lex. Stories and fables and tales have been banned since the Healing. My adventurous stitching was viewed by some as "fiction" and it sentenced me to the Ark. But this is different. "It's not fiction, Jasper. It's a reconstruction of her life based on the Relics I found," I say, sounding more defensive than I'd like.

"How could you do that, Eva?"

"What do you mean?"

He stands and points his finger at me. "I mean, how could you treat the Testing like this? The Lex tells us that the Chronicles are the way to teach the New North people about dangers of the pre-Healing world and to reinforce our community's decision to live in the Golden Ages. They don't merely serve to entertain." He spits out the last word as if it's blasphemy.

Perhaps he's raised his voice to attract the attention of the Climbers again. But I no longer care if we are overheard, and I no longer feel like some unprotected Maiden awaiting the verdict of her Gallant. I stand up and face him head on. "You haven't even read my Chronicle."

"I can't believe I supported your participation in the Testing. You've risked my success at the Testing—and our future Union—with this stunt."

"It sounds like you're mostly mad because I stand a chance at winning. Truly the behavior of a Gallant."

He stares at me for a long tick, and then storms off into the darkening night.

Part of me wants to race after him and scream at him for speaking to me that way. Part of me wants to stay far away from the camp, poisoned as it is now with Jasper and his words. It's clear that I have to sacrifice any chance with Jasper if I want to win. I also realize that—no matter what the Climber reported about the reaction to my Chronicle— many others in the Aerie may react just like Jasper.

I take a deep breath, and decide to do something else entirely. Something forbidden.

I pull out my harness from my pack, run a line through it, and thread it through my ice screw. Then I descend into the crevasse for one last visit with Elizabet.

XXXI

Aprilus 24
Year 242, A.H.

I can hardly see. Whether it's from the tears streaming down my face or the Sun as She fades, I'm not sure. But I don't care. I'm not going to let Jasper—or anyone else, for that matter—ruin my possibilities. I believe in my Chronicle. Given the choice I would still pick discovering Elizabet's belongings over an Apple Relic, with its greater certainty of winning the Tests. Even if I face reprisals. And I'm not going to let anyone rob me of a final *vale* to Elizabet or a fight for victory in honor of Lukas and Eamon.

Thank the Gods I know the crevasse so well I can belay down with my eyes closed. Which is what I do. Fighting off my instinct to focus my vision—a futile task, anyway—I let my hands and feet guide the way down to my Claim.

Within a few ticks, I've found my Claim stakes, still lodged in the ice wall. Only then do my eyelids flutter open.

Reaching for the *naneq* still hanging from a stake, I light it. I spot the hollow where I found Elizabet's pink pack. I run my gloved hand along the groove where I prised her belongings from the ice, and whisper the words of goodbye.

"*Vale in aeternam*, Elizabet."

The ice feels softer than I remember, probably from the warming spring air. My glove catches on a tiny fissure in the hollow's ice wall, one I don't recall seeing before. Maybe it surfaced as the upper layers melted. As I try to pull my glove out of the stubborn crack, I think I see a glint of metal. But this ice wall has played so many tricks on me over the past *siniks*, I've learned not to trust it.

The fissure won't let go, and it's getting darker by the tick. It almost feels like someone's gripping my hand. Even though we're not supposed to touch the Testing Site now that it's closed, I really have no choice but to grab a small pick out of my pack with my free hand and work away at the ice that has seized my glove. After I hack away, the cloth finally comes loose. I breath a huge sigh of relief; having made it this far, I certainly don't want to die on my final *sinik* of the Testing.

I'm about to start my climb back up, when that glimmer catches my eye again. I know I should ignore it, but I can't.

Crawling across to the spot, I hold my *naneq* close to the disrupted ice. I don't even need to grab a tool to dislodge the object. I can see it plain as day. My heart seizes. It's an Apple amulet. But there's more. It's hangs around the neck of a skeleton.

Is it Elizabet? Deep within myself, I know it is. It's too close to her precious pink pack to be anyone else. I start to cry again. What in the Gods should I do? This isn't just a skeleton; this is my Elizabet.

I scrape away the final layer of ice and caress her bony cheek. Poor, poor Elizabet, I can't leave her down here. I can't abandon her. But there's no way I can get her body out of the crevasse by myself. And since The Lex says once the Site is closed no Testors are allowed in and no one can remove Relics, how am I supposed to remove her from this icy grave? I can't.

Damn The Lex. I'm going to have to leave her here. Then it occurs to me. I don't have to leave *all* of her here, do I?

I grab my pick again, and remove the thin, wet layer of ice covering poor Elizabet's body. Touching her skeletal face gently, I unhook the Apple amulet off of her neck and slide it into my pack. Even if no one ever sees the amulet but me—only the Gods know what would happen to me if anyone found out I'd been here after the Site closure—I'll have this to remember her always.

With the outer layer of ice gone, I can see more. Elizabet has a flat, metal object folded into her arms. Holding the *naneq* a little closer, I realize just what it is. A diptych altar to Apple. The one Relic above all others. Last found one hundred and fifty years ago. The Pre-Healing people stared at its blank, glass surface as they worshipped. As they prayed in desperation. Hoping that Apple will give them some message, some sign.

Pushing aside my fear—this belonged to my Elizabet, after all—I wrest it from her bony arms as gently as I can. Too scared to do much more than slide it in my pack, I tell myself I'll look at it later. In the safety of my igloo. For now, I've got to get out of the crevasse before the blackness of night falls on me.

"Goodbye, Elizabet," I say, with a final touch on her cheek.

Her eyes can no longer see, but I feel her Spirit everywhere, watching me.

I scuttle back over to the base of my rope, hurl my large pick into the ice above my head, and dig my bear-claw boots into the wall-face. But I feel the rope begin to slip. The ice screw holding my line into place on the surface has lost its grip in the melting snow. I have only a tick before it's too late. Grabbing my *ulu* out of my belt, I unhook myself from my harness and sever the line before it falls into the bottomless crevasse, taking me along with it. The line and ice screw fly past me. In sick fascination, I watch and wait for the sound of them hitting bottom. No noise ever comes.

I am paralyzed with fear, staring down into the endless black. That could've been me, falling without end. *Move, Eva, move,* I tell myself, *or it will be you.* I cling to the face of the ice wall with my axe and my bear-claw boots, the only tools left to me. I have no choice but to climb back up, this time creeping inch by inch.

My progress is slow, hampered by the darkness. I have too many ticks to think about my stupidity. What was this all for? This final descent into the crevasse? For Elizabet? For anger over Jasper? Doesn't he deserve to win? What about the Testing? Did I do it only for Eamon? Did he even believe in the Testing at the time of his death? Do I believe now?

Eamon. The Ring. His death.

He and I stand together—hands linked across time, both incredibly foolhardy. Only he died.

I can't do that to my parents. I can't allow another Ring-Guard to deliver the broken body of another child to their doorstep. Remembering how crushed they were, how long it took for them to rebuild themselves as the Chief Archon and his Lady, and how doubtful I am that they'd be able to do so again, I realize that I must return to the Aerie by whatever means possible. Just as I promised my father the day I left for the Testing.

I will not let this crevasse or the Testing or my family or even The Lex defeat me. I will not doubt myself as Eamon did in the end: *will my family still love me when I do what I must?* I will survive, for Lukas and Eamon and Elizabet and myself. I'll pray that love will remain in the face of survival.

XXXII

Aprilus 24
Year 242, A.H.

The surface of the crevasse finally approaches. Uncertain how I'll hoist my exhausted body over the lip, I see that Jasper left an ice screw behind. Hooking the tip of my axe into the hole of the ice screw, I test its strength and then pull myself the final distance. Too tired to care if I get caught, I lay at the rim, panting.

I hear footsteps running toward me. "Are you all right?"

"I am now," I answer, without looking up. A hand reaches under my armpit and pulls me to standing. It's the white-haired Boundary Climber. Again. He's everywhere, it seems.

"You shouldn't have been down there. It's too dangerous." He's almost yelling at me.

"I know. The Lex prohibits it, and I'm sure the Scouts will

be thrilled when they hear about my Lex-breaking." I'm so exhausted I'm shaking, but a new energy courses through me. "They've been waiting all Testing."

"It's not that, Eva." He looks at the area around my Claim. "I mean, it's pitch-black down there and your ice screw pulled out of the *masak*. You could've been killed. He would kill me if anything happened to you."

"Who? Who would kill you?" Fear and sadness vanish. I wonder who would have possibly struck a deal with a Climber to protect me such that he would kill them if they failed. Until a few ticks ago, I might have suspected Jasper. Now I can only think of one person. Suddenly it all makes sense: the jealous glares, the hushed conversations, the resentment. I was never really in danger. "My father?"

The Climber looks away. "I can't . . . I'd get in trouble if you got killed in the crevasse. It's my job to make sure no one goes down there, right?"

I don't believe him, but I'm too tired to argue right now. And anyway, I don't think he'd tell me even if I insisted. "Right. Well, I guess you can take me back to the Scouts to face my punishment now."

"You aren't the only one who'd get punished, Eva."

"So you're not going to turn me in?"

"As long as you don't turn me in."

"It's a deal." I decide to try my luck. "Can I ask you one last question?"

"It depends on what it is."

"Were you telling the truth about the New North people liking my Chronicle?"

"I always tell the truth."

He gives me a little bow and walks off to continue his rounds. Legs wobbly, I walk the short distance back to camp. I skirt around the perimeter so no one watches my approach. Then I sidle into my igloo to examine my new Relics.

I peel off my sealskin outer coats and lay out my mat. Opening my pack, I pull out the Apple amulet first. The talisman is rectangular and black, with a small metallic square poking out of the bottom. I notice that the metallic square is hollow, as if designed to slide into another object like a puzzle piece. The amulet itself hangs on a long black cord, so Elizabet could wear it close to her heart.

Returning to my pack, I slide out the diptych. I run my fingers along its smooth silver surface, tracing the Apple image on top. I linger on the tiny bite taken out of the Apple symbol. I'm nervous. The Apple diptych is the most blasphemous and dangerous of any man-made object. The Triad seeks them above all other Relics so they can protect the people of New North from their dark powers. I run my fingers along the gap where the two sides of the diptych meet. I'm sure there must be an opening somewhere; our diptychs have a little catch where we can raise the top open. Feeling a little groove under my fingertip, I hook my nail on it. I've broken so many rules already, I feel as if I'm in a dream. I have no choice but to open this altar.

There it is. The notorious blank surface to which the pre-Healing people prayed. On the other side are little squares with letters and numbers. Did they write out their supplications to Apple this way? No one really knows. I wonder if Elizabet believed that Apple answered her. It saddens me to think of her spending her final ticks sending messages to a god that was false.

It feels wrong not to turn this over to the Triad. But what

are my choices? I can't divulge my discovery without also revealing that I broke The Lex and reentered the Site. Not only would I be disqualified from the Testing, I would risk severe punishment to the Climber, myself, and my family. The only Testor in the history of the Testing who entered a closed Site and tried to submit a late-found artifact was exiled to the Boundary lands—along with his family. I couldn't do that to my parents, make them give up the Founding status my family has held since the Healing and the Chief Archon title for which my father worked so hard. They've been through too much already. Only the Gods know what the Triad would do to the Climber.

I decide to keep the altar hidden for now.

Maybe the coming days will show me a way to share my discovery without bringing harm upon myself. But even if they don't, I feel a curious peace. They are a part of Elizabet, after all. Even if I lose, I want to keep a part of her with me always.

XXXIII

Aprilus 26 and 27
Year 242, A.H.

On the last night before we make the Passage into the Aerie, Jasper sits next to me at dinner, and I let him. For the past two *siniks*—since we left the Testing Site to return—I've sidestepped him. It's been easy; we've spent every waking hour speeding back through the wilderness toward home. But my anger toward him has mellowed a little. And my curiosity has mounted, even though I tell myself it doesn't matter. What does Jasper still want with me? When he clearly thinks so little of me? Has he re-thought his harsh judgment about my Chronicle? The judgment I now fear will be shared by the Aerie people, including the Triad?

Jasper doesn't say anything at first. He doesn't eat anything. He doesn't even pretend to.

I let my thoughts return to the disturbing observations I've made since we left the Testing Site. The return journey is amazingly short. All we have to do is navigate our teams over a fixed, well-worn path obviously familiar to Scouts and Boundary Fishermen and Hunters alike. None of my fellow Testors seem to notice the incongruity of it all, not even Jasper. It's surreal. The fact that the journey could've been so easy—that we needn't have risked, and lost, so much—makes me furious in a different way. The Testing seems more and more like a cruel inside joke understood only by a select few. No matter that The Lex itself—and through it, the Gods—sanctifies it. Is this what Eamon discovered? That the sacred has been corrupted? Maybe mankind hasn't changed all that much since the Healing.

Jasper clears his throat, interrupting my dark thoughts.

"Eva," he whispers, "I'm sorry."

I don't answer. If he's expecting me to fall over backward in forgiveness, he's wrong. The wound he left is way too deep. Instead, I keep eating.

"I messed up. I shouldn't have talked like that to you."

He sounds genuine, but there's something missing in his apology. I don't hear him say that he thinks he was wrong. I have to know what he really believes.

"Do you believe the things you said to me were wrong? Or do you think they're true, and you're just sorry you actually said them to me? Because I'm a Maiden, or something equally stupid."

Jasper pauses. He seems a little stumped by my question. Then he says, "That's kind of hard to answer, Eva. I mean, The Lex states we are to use Relics to teach, not tell stories. But I also know how good you are and how dedicated you are to fulfilling the Testing's purpose—just like Eamon.

RELIC: THE BOOKS OF EVA

I guess I'm having a hard time making sense of how The Lex's words could fit your actions. It makes me confused about the Testing, actually."

I resist the urge to reach out. Most Gallants would just spout off some flowery language to appease me. Not to mention, he's taking a big risk by making such a confession—questioning The Lex at all is tantamount to breaking it. More than that, I share his confusion about The Lex, the Testing, his role, our relationship, everything. Has he been feeling the same way as me all along?

"Thanks, Jasper."

He looks surprised. "For what? I know I didn't offer you the right kind of apology, the Gallant kind."

"For being honest."

We sit quietly for a few long ticks. The fire crackles and the busy hum of the camp takes the place of our discussion. I push my food around on my plate. I don't know what to say next. And I'm afraid of what he might say.

Jasper flashes me that bright smile of his. Then he leans forward and whispers, "It would be an honor to have an Archon in the family. Whoever it turns out to be."

XXXIV

Aprilus 28
Year 242, A.H.

Our return to the Aerie is so different from our departure. A huge ceremonial procession, complete with flying red banners and a phalanx of Scouts and Boundary Climbers and Attendants: we travel as one. We are no longer a bunch of scared eighteen-year-olds, sent out for the Gods to choose an Archon; we are a fierce pack of returning survivors. Or we play those roles, anyway.

With each step, my heart pounds faster. The amulet and altar seem to grow heavier in my pack. The Ring looks enormous from the outside. Without the ice and stone buildings of the Aerie to soften it, it rises up from the ice flats of the Boundary lands like a tower jutting toward the heavens. Precisely as The Lex describes it. I feel as though the Ring is judging me from on high, almost like one of the Gods. I silently pray that the New North people adjudicate me more kindly than the Ring appears to, and that they don't make me into an example for trying something so risky with my Chronicle.

Our entire procession has stopped at a makeshift camp just outside the Ring. Testors and Scouts alike pause to prepare before we make the Passage. As they do, they chatter about the Testing and their chances. I catch loads of references to Jasper, but no one mentions me. The Climber must have been lying about the people's reaction to my Chronicle. He was probably having fun at my expense; maybe he even knew that I stood to be punished for my Chronicle and mocked me.

How could I have ever thought that Aleksandr and Neil saw me as a threat? And why did I imagine that Scout Okpik harbored secret hatred toward me? He's ignored me for a long while now. It was my father all along, pulling strings so I would survive. It must have been.

Watching this group—especially stalwart Scouts like Okpik—frenzied to clean their filthy sealskin coats and pants and wash their faces for the first time in many *siniks*, I almost laugh aloud. But then I remember what awaits on the other side of the Ring, and the laughter disappears. I figure that I should look as presentable as possible—even Maidenly, if I can—to confront the Triad and the masses. Secretly, I pull out the mirror Relic to get a glimpse of myself. I badly need to scrub my own face and brush out my tangled bird's nest of hair.

The people of New North have begun to assemble. An advance Scout has been sent to alert them to our Passage and, from years of Testing, I know they will hurry away from their daily tasks to secure the best spot for watching our triumphant return. And the Selection Ceremony, of course, where only the Gods know what will happen.

My stomach jumps at the thought of all those faces staring at me, assessing me. My mother and father, of course. My teachers and schoolfriends, the few that stuck by me. People I will not recognize except by profession—Builder, Blacksmith, Tailor, Baker—the list goes on. Maybe even my old Nurse Aga, whom I haven't seen for years.

What will all those people think of me looking like this? What will Lukas? Lukas, if I can make him out in the back of the crowds where the Boundary people watch alongside the Attendants. Will he be upset with me for not following his instructions to the letter? Will he be offended by my Chronicle? Will he be upset if I lose out to Jasper?

How will New North judge me?

The horns bellow. I say goodbye to my beloved dog team before handing them off to Boundary Attendants; I'll miss them in the *siniks* ahead. They have been the only constant in the Testing, Indica especially. But I make sure to keep my pack on my back. Only the Gods know what would happen to me if the people knew what I was hiding. Something far worse than the judgment I might receive for writing my Chronicle.

We assemble in line just behind the Gate to the Aerie. Jasper stands two Testors ahead of me—Thurstan and Benedict are between us—and he makes a special point to glance back and smile. It comforts. No matter what happens on this *sinik* and all the *siniks* to come, I believe he'll be a friend first and last. At that very tick, we begin to make the Passage. As we traverse the arched stone that divides the Boundary lands from the Aerie town square, I am awestruck by the crowds. After so many *siniks* of solitude and ice, the numbers overwhelm; they remind me of the crush of people Elizabet faced when she tried to escape to the docks. I glance around, looking for familiar faces, but there are too many people to separate just one from the masses.

We continue our procession to the stage. There the Selection Ceremony will commence in a bell or less. As we march, I notice a murmur coming from the crowds. It grows in volume, and by the Gods, it sounds like they're chanting.

"*Eva . . . Eva . . . Eva . . .*"

But that can't be right. Why would they be calling my name?

My stomach sinks. Is the chant linked to some judgment the Triad will be issuing about my Chronicle? It doesn't sound as harsh as the Punishment Chants, but maybe because I am so afraid. The stage suddenly looks less like a place where I'll be receiving the Archon Laurels, and more like a place where I'll be sentenced.

One by one, we mount the austere wooden platform. Scanning the town square, I'm struck by how small—and cramped—the Aerie seems compared to the vast fields of snow and the endless sea outside the Ring. Why are we all mashed in here when there's so much space and air on our doorstep? I want to run away.

My legs shake. Near the front of the crowds, I see my parents. Tiny tears stream down my father's otherwise stoic face, and he reaches his two fingers up to his lips, as if to kiss me from afar. Is he kissing me goodbye? I look over at my mother for some sign as to how to read my father's face. My mother's face is frozen into her public smile, an expression that could mean just about anything.

Where is Lukas? I need to see him. I had hoped my parents would let him stand alongside them, even though he's Boundary-born and I know he's due to be sent back to the Boundary lands since his work as a Companion is over. Finally, I spot him. In the far back, over a sea of black-haired Boundary heads, he stands in the exact same place as the day I left. He, too, is unreadable. I start to mouth a question to him—to ask him what in the Gods is going on—but he shakes his head.

What is going to happen to me?

The town square bell chimes once. The crowd hushes. We all stand in silent reverence until the full twelve chimes sound—one for each Testor, returned and fallen. As we wait, a thousand torches are lit to a full blaze in a circle around the town square.

The Chief Triad—Lexor, Basilikon, and Archon—join us on the stage, their Triad symbols emblazoned on their chests. The Testors are supposed to kneel for the Chief Basilikon's blessing and the anointment of Healing waters, but my body is locked in fear. An Assistant Basilikon has to place his hand on my shoulder in order for my paralysis to unlock.

After the blessing, we rise. The Chief Lexor begins to speak—Ian, Jasper's uncle. I wonder if he's going to utter the words used in every Selection Ceremony I've ever seen or render my judgment. I hope it's the latter because I can hardly stand to wait another tick.

"Today, we gather for the *Salve*, the welcome greeting for our returned Testors."

The words are familiar, but the crowd erupts. This reaction is unusual. No matter the people's feelings about the Testors' homecoming, they usually respect the solemnity of the occasion. After all, Testors perish beyond the Ring. Tristan and Anders did.

Ian raises his hand to quiet them. They settle down, but a final holdout shouts, "Eva!" Why? Is he clamoring for my punishment? Does he suspect my father rigged the Testing so I would survive? The other Testors are confused as well; they keep glancing over at me. I feel certain that all my suspicions are becoming reality.

"These brave Testors have returned to the safety of the Aerie from a journey to the most hazardous part of New North—the Frozen Shores. This dangerous expedition claimed the lives of two of our brave young men: Testor Tristan and Testor Anders." He repeats verbatim the sacred words I heard out in the wild: "While we lament the loss of our brothers, we know that the Gods will welcome Tristan and Anders into their realm. For they lost their lives in the sacred trial of the Testing, which the Gods themselves sanctified in The Lex for the good of mankind after the Healing. We raise our hands in prayer for Tristan and Anders."

Ian raises his hands to the sky in supplication. The people lift their hands and eyes to the heavens as The Lex requires, although real tears stream down many of their faces. I'm sure the lost Testors were known to many of them, and the people's sadness reminds me once again of the senselessness of Tristan and Anders' deaths. We could have taken safer routes to the Frozen Shores, and we need not have ventured out alone—*were it not for some leader's mistaken notion of what The Lex demands*, I think. I suspect the same thought crossed Eamon's mind.

Ian turns back to us. "The Gods saw fit to return these fine young Testors to us. They placed themselves in the gravest of dangers for our benefit, to become Archons. We of New North need Archons to show us the perils of our ways before the Healing. Together and again, we reject the worship of the false god Apple. We reject his Tylenols and Cokes and MasterCards. We reject all the Relics the Testors have discovered and have yet to discover. Those standing before us have unearthed from the ice Relics unseen since the days of the Healing—Relics that will show us the rightness of New North's ways. And they have created Chronicles about their Relics that sanctify the ways of The Lex. "

We stand.

The Chief Archon—my father—takes center stage. It is his turn to speak.

He nods at Ian, and begins. "This year, our Testors discovered some of the finest—and rarest—Relics in our history. As many of you know from our town square Gatherings, they have unearthed unnatural remedies, Earth-damaging engines, vile weapons, and even a small worship tablet to the false god Apple—one that ruled mankind's lives in the final pre-Healing days. And as you all know from the Gatherings, some of our Testors have fashioned very powerful Chronicles for their Relics. We will celebrate each Testor singularly."

My father's voice simultaneously soothes and terrifies. I love hearing his familiar tones again—after so long beyond the Ring—but I dread what he might say next. He's made no mention of the heresy of my Chronicle. Not yet, anyway. Will he dole out my judgment when my name is called in turn? This waiting is cruel punishment in and of itself. Especially if my father must dispense it.

My father calls out each Testor. I stand, my legs quaking, as each of the other nine remaining Testors listens to a description of their Relics and a summary of their Chronicle. We hear about Jacques' box of remedies; the silver-foiled foodstuffs found by Benedict, Petr, and Thurstan; William's metallic nets; the guns unearthed by Aleksander and Neils; and Knud's modest cache of fishing lures. And of course, Jasper's Apple Relic which receives the most applause.

What about me? My mouth moves in silent prayers to the Gods. The Sun especially, for She is known for Her mercy.

The Chronicles are not re-read in full as most people do not need to hear them again. If I wasn't so scared, I would've wanted to hear every word, to see how the other Testors' histories compare to my own. How my Relics and Chronicle stack up against the others. But I have bigger concerns than winning now. I am last. It seems forever until I am called.

"Testor Eva, please come forward."

A murmuring in the crowd surges until it becomes nearly a roar. The sound unnerves me, as I pad across the stage in my threadbare *kamiks*. My father has to steady me when I take my place at his side. For a brief tick, his hands touch my pack, and I flinch, thinking of its secrets: the amulet and altar. I can only imagine the reaction when I'm passed to the Guards for punishment and they find my contraband.

He gives me the tiniest of smiles, undetectable by the rest of New North I'm sure. Then the Chief Archon mask descends, and his voice booms across the town square. "Testor Eva, you made a prodigious find."

A prodigious find. That doesn't sound like a damning judgment. Not yet. I hold my breath.

"You found a pink pack full of Relics evidencing the sad depravity of the pre-Healing lifestyle." He lists the items in Elizabet's pack. They sound soulless when described in his ritual tone; I hear none of the life I found sparking within them.

He continues. "But your Chronicle of those Relics proved to be, well, more powerful than the Relics alone. If you had been standing on this stage when your Chronicle was read aloud, you would have heard nothing but silence."

By the Gods. My Chronicle must have shocked New North into silence. Surely it's the time for my judgment. Before, I'd wished that he would ease my suffering and announce my sentence immediately, but now I want more time to plan an escape. I scan the crowds and the Ring-walls looking for way to break free. If I could just make it through the Gate to my dog team, I know I could survive beyond the Ring . . .

I half-hear my father continue. "Eva, you would have heard silence followed by cheers. Silence to commemorate Elizabet Laine and a life lost to the Healing, and cheers for you in recognizing the story in her Relics and capturing it so we could understand."

I whirl from the crowds and stare at him. Did he really just say what I think I he said? Did he actually just compliment me for my rogue Chronicle? In his role as Chief Archon, not my father?

"It is time!" he calls out.

The thousand torches are abruptly extinguished. Although it is still day, the Aerie town square becomes dark under the cloudy, late afternoon sky. My father lights the single torch on the stage and then, unrolls the scroll he has held in his hand since he stepped onto the stage.

"The Gods have made their decision. The new Archon is Eva."

XXXV

Aprilus 28
Year 242, A.H.

I pass from person to person like a baby on her Water-naming day. I hardly feel the hands and the arms and lips on my cheek. I am numb and reeling simultaneously. I wonder if I'll ever feel normal again. Did I really just win the Archon Laurels?

It seems impossible. True, I'd harbored aspirations of winning. I even once believed that I stood a chance. But after Jasper's discovery and after I realized that the novelty of my Chronicle might backfire upon me, I stopped fantasizing about victory and started worrying about the very real possibility of punishment. Anyway, even if I hadn't written such a risky Chronicle, who was I to seek the Laurels? The first Maiden Testor in one hundred and fifty years? A girl who hadn't started training until three months before the Testing? Mother was right to be dismissive.

But something swayed the odds in my favor. What was it?

Just as I finish extricating myself from the suffocating embrace of my father's aunt, Jasper approaches with his parents. I'm not sure what to expect, no matter his "happy to have an Archon in the family" remark. Everything has changed. I watch as my parents straighten their Feast-day clothes; clearly, they're a little apprehensive too.

The Lex demands that our parents speak first, and I'm relieved. Even though Jasper is smiling at me, I wouldn't want to utter anything foolish in this dicey situation.

My father bows to Jasper's parents. "We thank the Gods that they returned Jasper and Eva home to us safely. We are blessed, as two Testors were lost in the Lex-sanctified quest."

Jasper's mother nods in acceptance of his words, clever in their focus on our safe homecoming. It was the only prayer that my father had offered on our last night in the Aerie, when our two families were gathered together.

The iciness of Jasper's mother is apparent, but she knows better than to say what she really thinks. That I'd robbed her precious son of what should be his—of a title that someone in every generation of her family had held since the Healing. That I don't deserve it. That the Triad should never have let a female compete in the first place. She wouldn't dare utter such statements in front of the Chief Archon. Or me, now.

"You will come to our home afterward? To Feast with us?" my father asks.

She cannot say no. It would do me dishonor as the new Archon—and my father as Chief Archon. Not to mention that my father didn't insult her by explicitly inviting her to celebrate my victory. Just our homecoming.

Jasper is still beaming at me. He's acting truly happy with my victory, not upset by his own loss like so many despondent Testors around us. I'd like to believe that he's the friend I'd been hoping he was. But I wonder what's really behind that smile.

Our meeting is interrupted by a visit from Ian and the Chief Basilikon. Jasper and his family bow to their relative and then take their leave, while my mother and I do a deep curtsy. The once-automatic gesture feels strange in my stiff and filthy Testor uniform. My pack weighs me down as I bend—but I strive for Maidenly grace.

"You should be very proud of your Eva," Ian commands rather than observes, using the full power of his Chief Lexor voice.

"She has done honor to the Gods, and her family," my father answers, and I swell with pride at his words.

"Her Chronicle was most powerful," the Chief Basilkon says, echoing my father's words on the stage. I can't quite tell if he's praising me, or begrudgingly accepting my victory, or lying about the whole thing. Maybe he itched for punishment instead of Laurels, but he has some secret reason for publicly forgiving my impropriety. My father's position, maybe? I can't help but think about Eamon's words from his journal—*I can no longer ignore the truth of what I've learned.* Had he learned something about the Chief Basilkon? Something that would compel the Basilikon to excuse the irregularity of my Chronicle? Perhaps so he can hold me under his sway?

"Enjoy your thirty days with her. After that, she'll be off for her Archon training," Ian directs. As if he could order happiness.

My father places his arm around me. "We've already planned. We will relish every tick."

The other two chiefs of the Triad turn to leave. My parents and I assume our genuflections and curtsies. Then, arms linked, we head home.

The walk, which once seemed quite long, is but a few steps. In ticks, we are through the door. Everything seems impossibly luxurious after so many days on dogsleds and in crevasses, so many nights in igloos and tents. Especially since the tables of the solar and dining room—heaped high with fruit, beautifully sculpted breads and cakes, roasted fish and fowl—are already laid out for a great Feast.

"How did you know?" I ask.

"What do you mean, Eva?" my father asks back.

"How did you know that I'd win? You said 'we've already planned.' Even though you're the Chief Archon, you couldn't have possibly known that I'd be named the new Archon and thrown together a Feast of this magnitude just today. And if it's been Jasper that had won, his family would be holding the Feast today."

My parents shoot each other an inscrutable glance. My mother answers, "Eva, it seemed impossible that you should lose. You can't imagine how you moved the New North people with your Chronicle at the Gatherings. We had never heard so wrenching a tale of the end. That poor girl."

The contraband in my pack reminds me of something. I carefully extricate my father's Relic: the mirror that earned him the role of Chief Archon. "I would have met my end were it not for this," I say, my voice hoarse. "Thank you for allowing me to take it."

My father nods solemnly and replaces the mirror on its spot on the mantle, faced toward the Sun. "Eva, the Gods have blessed you with a special gift. To see the hidden truth that lay within the Relics. And to tell that truth so power-fully. No other Testor has ever had that talent. Not in the entire history of the Testing."

My eyes well with tears. He speaks of truth, but he means stories. My mind turns to Nurse Aga at whose feet I began to learn storytelling. I step close to them. I am awestruck by their compliments. "Truly?"

"Truly," my father answers.

"Truly," my mother echoes, with a sniff.

I think she's holding back tears. But I see a grimace. For the first time in *siniks*, it registers that I've spent too long in these exact same clothes. In the warmth and closeness of the stone building, I realize the problem: I don't smell Maidenly.

"Eva, you really must bathe before our Guests arrive for the Feast," my mother manages in her whispery Lady voice. She can only hold back her Lady ways for so long.

My father glances my way, and nods. "That would be wise, Eva. I noticed your—umm—aroma in the town square. I didn't want to embarrass you before we arrived home."

I laugh. After all that I've faced these past twenty-eight *siniks*—body-wrenching cold, hunger, suspected conspir-acy against me, near-death drops—the last thing I thought about was how I smelled. Yet back at the Aerie, it's one of the first things I've got to tackle. My shoulders slump in relief. I am home. "I'm hardly embarrassed, Father. I would love nothing more than a long, hot bath." I also welcome the excuse to lock myself in my bedroom and hide the amulet and altar that I've been carrying.

My mother smiles. Not only have I stepped into her realm, I am happily agreeing to her suggestions. For once. "I've already ordered your Companion Katja to prepare it."

Katja? I'd almost forgotten about her.

I turn to give my parents a hug before racing upstairs, but something makes me hesitate. I'm excited and relieved to see them, but everything feels just a little too easy. Their Feast preparations, the Archon Laurels, Jasper's amiable reaction. So I give them a smile and a wave. Still, my own stench reminds me that I am Maiden once again. I must also keep the stench of my secrets hidden.

XXXVI

Aprilus 28
Year 242, A.H.

"Give me a tick," I call at the knock on my bedroom door. I assume it's Katja. Earlier in the day, I had dismissed her so I could be alone in my room and bath; my *siniks* outside the Ring taught me to relish solitude. But now, with the guests beginning to arrive for the Feast, she's probably eager to see if I need any help before I head downstairs.

I've got to be quick and hide the altar and amulet; I couldn't resist looking at them once I was alone. The compulsion to make Elizabet real again was much too strong. I slide the altar back into my pack and bury it the bottom of a pile of smelly Testing garments. Until I find a suitable hiding spot, I figure that the smell and grime alone will keep the altar safe from everyone tonight, including Katja, whom

I instructed not to touch them. Then I hang the amulet around my neck and tuck it beneath my Feast dress. I want to have Elizabet close to me—it's her night, too. Looking down, I'm pleased that the sumptuous pattern my mother embroidered on the gown's bodice masks the amulet. I must remember to thank my mother for the elaborate new dress; she must have worked on it the entire time I was gone.

"Come in," I yell.

The door opens. But it's not Katja. It's Lukas.

I stand up and grin crazily. Grasping onto his hands, I blurt out, "I've been wanting to speak with you since I saw you in the town square. How can I thank you for all you taught me? I could never have survived without you, let alone won. You were with me beyond the Ring, Lukas. Every tick."

He smiles back, his grip tight and warm. "Thank you, Eva, but you did it yourself. I'm so happy you won the Laurels, but most of all, I'm happy you're home."

"Me, too," I said.

We grow quiet. There's so much I want to say, but I hardly know where to begin. Maybe he feels the same way. Or maybe it's just the Boundary quietude in him.

"I've come to say goodbye, Eva."

"Goodbye? I've only just returned. I've got thirty more days here at home before I have to go study with the Archons. I wanted to go over every detail of the Testing with you."

He lets go of me. "It's not you that's leaving. It's me. Your parents were kind to let me stay until you got back. Tomorrow, I go home to the Boundary lands. Until my re-assignment, at least."

"No! I have so much I want to talk with you about. How can they do that?"

"It is their right within The Lex, Eva. You know that. They did me a kindness to let me stay so long. So I could attend the Gathering every day, to hear about your progress."

I know he's right, even though it seems unfair. On impulse, I hug him. He is stiff at first. But then he relents and hugs me back. As we separate, I notice a corner of the Apple altar peeking out from my pack at the bottom of the sealskin heap. I must not have closed up the pack all the way. Surreptitiously, I try to kick it back under the pile.

"What is that, Eva?"

"Just some junk from my Testing gear."

He tries to walk toward it, but I stand between him and the pile. "I wouldn't get too close. My Testing clothes don't smell too fresh." I try to distract him with a joke.

As he leans over to touch the altar, I pull away his hand. "Stop, Lukas," I warn him.

It's only the third time I've ever ordered him to do anything, even though he's technically my servant. Behind his usual mask, his eyes flicker with disbelief.

When he tries again, I lunge for the altar and clutch it in my arms. I can feel the altar gleam in the lamplight of my bedroom, surreal and almost magical amidst the ice-solid world of the Aerie. Lukas is staring at it.

"It's an Apple altar, isn't it?" he whispers.

"How do you know?" Very few people have ever seen one, even in a textbook. And Lukas doesn't read our Latin.

"I know a lot more about Apple altars than you think."

I glare at him. All of a sudden he feels like a stranger. Yet I am more angry at him than scared of his terrifying boast. "Like what?"

"It wouldn't be safe for me to tell you. Please turn it over, Eva."

"No. It's mine. I mean, it was Elizabet's. And I can't turn it over to the Triad because I didn't find it until the Testing was already over. You know what they could do to me."

He turns to me, his eyes sharp. "I don't mean for you to turn it over to the Triad. I mean for you to turn it over to me, Eva. Please." Despite his use of the word "please," he isn't asking me. He is commanding me.

I step away from him. Why is he speaking to me this way? "You? Why would I give it to you? If anyone, I should give it to the Triad."

He draws very, very close to me. His chest and broad shoulders are an ice wall. "Don't you understand that I am acting for your own safety? Have I ever asked you to do anything that wasn't for your protection?"

I shake my head, unable to speak.

"Then please trust me."

"I'm not the same naive Maiden who left for the Testing, Lukas," I whisper. "I'm stronger than I was before and smarter, too. I'm not going to just hand this Apple altar over to you just because you protected me in the past. I want a reason."

Lukas hesitates. "That Apple altar isn't what you think it is, Eva. If you let me have it until a bell after dawn, I promise you that I will reveal its secrets to you. Elizabet's secrets."

Elizabet's secrets? What in the Gods is he talking about?

I hear my father yell up the stairs. "Eva, your guests await you."

I am at a loss. I need to understand what Lukas is talking about, but I know if I don't go downstairs right now, someone will come up after me. And they'll stumble upon so many violations of The Lex that I'll be stripped of my victory and sentenced to death. I want to trust Lukas.

Eamon trusted him implicitly. I relied on Lukas utterly in the Testing.

Then again, I trusted Jasper, and he turned out to be less than completely honest with me. And now Lukas, who's been the only reliable presence in my life, suddenly possesses secret and blasphemous knowledge. But more disturbing, he seems very afraid for me, more afraid than he ever was when we prepared for the Testing. And the stakes are incredibly high; this is Elizabet and her Apple altar that we're talking about. So I ask him the one question for which I still have time.

"Are you suggesting that my Chronicle was wrong?" I ask.

"I wish that was all, Eva."

XXXVII
Aprilus 28
Year 242, A.H.

I descend the stairs to the solar with a heavy heart. I wanted to feel light and joyful, if only for this one night. Now that Lukas has the Apple altar, he has taken any possibility of joy from me. Maybe forever. But the Feast awaits and I slip back into my Maiden role, as if I'd never gone beyond the Ring. I smile demurely at the compliments of my aunts and uncles. I kneel for the Basilikon's blessing with the anointed Healing waters. I stand by as glass after glass of mead is lifted in toasts to my victory. I watch as our guests shovel mouthfuls of glorious abundant food into themselves. And I stand by and listen to my Relics and my Chronicle become legend.

It sounds as if everyone believes they know my Elizabet. They talk about her life so proprietarily, as if she was their discovery instead of mine. It bristles, and I unconsciously touch the amulet hidden under my dress bodice.

"Is there a fray in the stitching, dear?" My mother asks. Nothing escapes her prying eyes. I'd been so distracted by my encounter with Lukas that I'd forgotten to thank my mother for the gown. "Oh no, Mother. It's gorgeous. How can I thank you?"

"Just being here today, looking so lovely and alive, is my thanks," she says, very kindly and gently. So unlike her old self.

I feel a sudden surge of sympathy for my mother, and I squeeze her hand tight. "Well, I do thank you. I feel like a true Lady."

She smiles and squeezes my hand back. "You look like one."

The Feast conversation grows lively, and my mother and I turn to a very animated Jasper. He's regaling the guests with tales from the Testing, injecting levity into moments I remember more darkly. I take a tick to steal a glance at Lukas. He stands against the wall with the other Attendants as if nothing passed between us, just waiting to serve us as if it were any other day. How can he be so implacable, when my own stomach roils and my heart pounds at the thought of Elizabet's secrets? Should I really have trusted him enough to hand over my Apple altar? I can't go back now.

I hear the words "musk ox" being bandied about, and it catches my attention. Seeing my gaze, Jasper smiles at me, and continues his story, "So, I watch as Eva hauls the thing out the Taiga by herself. A musk ox!"

One of my aunts gasps. Our other guests squeal in laughter at the thought of Maidenly Eva dragging one of New

North's hugest creatures out of the forest, alone. I smile along with them, but it feels strange. Almost as if the Testing had been created solely for New North's entertainment. I wonder what the families of Tristan and Anders are doing right now. Surely not laughing.

The Attendants serve honey and fruit and cakes, usually my favorites. I'm sure my mother ordered them as a special treat for me, but they taste too sweet. False on my tongue. I push the delicacies around on my plate until the bell before the Evensong rings.

All the guests rise, even the Lexors, Archons, and Basilikons who don't need to leave follow the bells. I guess everyone in New North is used to having their days structured by the *Campana*. As I take my place at the front door to say my farewell, I realize that everyone's waiting in line to receive *my* blessings—not my father's. In the course of one day, power has shifted from my father to me. Me. Eva. It's too weird.

When the front door finally closes, I collapse into my father's waiting arms.

"You must be exhausted, dearest. Why don't you go to bed? Tomorrow will be time enough for us to talk about the future."

"The future? I thought my future was pretty well set. You know, being an Archon and all."

"Well, there's Jasper to consider now, too," he says.

I've just won the Archon Laurels, and they're already talking about my marriage prospects? I'm not exactly surprised, but it's a bit overwhelming right now. Especially since I have no idea how I feel about Jasper beyond friendship. "Jasper? I can't even think about that—"

"Of course not, Eva," my mother interjects. "There will

be plenty of time to consider Jasper's offer in the days to come."

Offer. The word spins in my brain. Has one already been made? I don't dare ask. I'm not ready for the details.

My mother hands me off to Katja. "Please get Eva settled in her bed. She needs her rest for the days ahead."

I start up the stairs, when my father calls out, "One last hug, Eva?"

Perhaps he's aware of the power shift, too. Perhaps he wants one last moment to think of me as his little girl. I race back down the steps into my father's arms. Only then do I realize that Lukas has been standing alongside the solar wall, listening to our conversation the entire time.

XXXVIII

Aprilus 28 and 29
Year 242, A.H.

How can I sleep? I'm bone-tired, but my mind won't rest. What is Lukas going to tell me? That the Testing is a sham, and that Eamon meant to challenge it? I've already started believing that myself. Or is it something else entirely?

Not for one more tick can I sit in this claustrophobic bedroom, doing nothing. I can't take the heat anymore; my body has grown too accustomed to deep cold. I slip on my *kamiks* and put my sealskin cloak on top of my nightdress. Slowly, I creak open my bedroom door and check the corridor. No one stirs in the house, so I tiptoe down the hall to the turret doorway.

The heavy wooden door groans when I push it open. I stiffen, certain that someone will wake up and catch me. But

I hear nothing, so I proceed. My *kamiks* glide up the familiar spiral stairwell, and I settle onto the hard stone bench lining the turret wall. The night is blue and still and cold, but not nearly as frigid as what I've felt outside the Aerie. I wrap my sealskin cloak around me like a blanket, and within a few ticks I'm comfortable enough. I spend the bells recording the past days in this journal.

When dawn comes and daybreak crests over the turret wall, I'm waiting.

Lukas jumps when he sees me. "How long have you been out here, Eva?"

"Not long. A few bells," I lie as I stand up to face him.

"That's long enough on a frigid night like this."

"Not when you've been beyond the Ring, Lukas."

"You're right. Sometimes I forget that you were really out there." He looks a little sad. As if it was somehow his fault that I'd entered the Testing. But I have no more patience for his so-called "secrets."

"What do you have to tell me? About my Apple altar?"

"I think it might be better seen than told."

Lukas is still making no sense, and I'm furious. "Are you deliberately trying to confuse me? Do you know what I'm risking?"

"Of course. But you have to understand: this isn't what you think. You were taught in School that this is a diptych, a folding altarpiece like many New North people keep in their homes to pray to their Gods. Except, supposedly the pre-Healing people used this to pray to the false god Apple, instead. Right?"

"Right." Why is he stating the obvious? Something every Schoolchild in the Aerie knows?

"It's actually something called a computer."

"A computer?" I've never heard the term before. Now he's speaking gibberish.

"It's a Tech device through which the pre-Healing people received images and information."

"Where they received information from the false god Apple?"

Altar in hand, Lukas moves closer to me. "No, Eva. It's a device were they received images and information from other pre-Healing people. They didn't use it to pray. They used it to communicate. Like we do by carrier pigeon. It's hard to explain, so maybe I should just show you." He starts opening the altar and pressing its edges.

"What are you doing?" I gasp. Instinctively I reach for it. I don't like him handling it so roughly.

Lukas gently moves my hand away. "Turning it on." He tears his gaze away from the altar to look at me. "Eva, this device captures power from the sun. I've been charging it since dawn. Just watch."

I stand next to him so I can get a better view of the altar's face. I still have absolutely no idea what he means by "on," but I figure I should wait and see. In a few ticks, the face of the altar begins to come alive with a jumble of color. I stifle a scream and jump back. It's evil, just like we've been taught. It has powers not of the Gods—not the Earth or Sun or Moon—nor The Lex. This is Tech. I have a terrible premonition that just by witnessing its power, I will die.

Lukas reaches out a hand to steady me. "There's nothing to be afraid of Eva. This is what I meant about turning the computer 'on.' In a few ticks, we'll see what kind of images it stores."

I have no choice but to stare. I am too paralyzed with

fear. The face turns bright blue. Pictures of the constellations begin to appear on it. How can the nighttime sky be appearing on this thing? It makes no sense. Without realizing, I reach out to touch it. To see if it's real.

Lukas grabs my hand before I make contact. "Don't. After all that time in the ice, it's pretty delicate. We don't want to break it before we see what's inside."

"We're going to open it up?"

"No. I don't mean actually *opening* it. We'll look at the screen."

"The screen?" All these new terms are making my head spin. How does Lukas know all this? And why hasn't he ever said anything about these things before?

"What you'd call the face of the altar," he clarifies. He begins to press on some small squares on the other side of the altar, and after a tick or so, a rectangle appears on the face. He taps on the altar again, and Elizabet's image emerges.

"By the Gods, it's Elizabet!" I'm so excited to see her face that I nearly forget the terror. Lukas clamps a hand over my mouth, but I'm squealing underneath his fingers.

"I want to see her," I mumble.

"Will you keep quiet?"

I nod, and Lukas removes his hand. I stare at the image. The blonde hair, light eyes, and sinewy limbs are exactly the same as all the pictures in her pink pack.

"It's really her. She looks just like the images in the Kirov Ballet book," I say.

"Would you like to hear Elizabet speak?"

"Speak? You can make her speak?" I sound like a child. I feel like one. It's as if my wish to make Elizabet come alive is becoming true.

The ever-humble Lukas puffs up a little. "I think so. Let me try."

He presses some squares again, and she moves. Her voice is shaky, and although her English is accented, her words are articulate and clear. She speaks directly to the computer. And there are tears running down her face. *"Robert, are you out there? It's me, Elizabet. I'm just praying that you get this post. Our connections have been getting weaker as the ocean waters have risen. Do you have any Internet connection left? I haven't received anything from you since last night. . ."*

I've stopped breathing. The world has shrunk to this miraculous vision.

Elizabet pauses to wipe the tears away from her eyes. Her eyes are bright, and very blue. *"My kultanen, I saved your message."* She rubs the amulet around her neck. *"Here, so I can keep it close to my heart. No matter what happens. The captain finally told me where we are going. Our course is due north, once we make it to the North Sea from the Baltic Sea, that is. We are heading for some obscure island in the Arctic, a place the captain says will be safe from the rising ocean waters. My family supposedly will be waiting for me there."*

Shaking her head, Elizabet says, *"I'm still trying to make sense of what he told me. I mean, how did my family know to go to this Arctic island? How do they know it's safe? The melting of the polar ice caps happened so suddenly. What would make them leave the safety of their Finnish palace almost a week before the catastrophe started? The captain said that my dad and the men from some of these other families were there because they'd been working on a joint venture oil project on this Arctic island. But that still doesn't explain the timing."*

I turn to Lukas, wide-eyed, but he raises a finger to his lips, his brow furrowed in concentration.

Elizabet laugh a little ruefully. *"But you know me, I didn't want to leave the Kirov until the last possible second. I just had to debut the La Bayadere at the Mariinsky Theater, Armageddon or not. I just had to secure that glory and fame, didn't I? Stupid, huh? Stubborn, at best."* The laughter stops. *"Did you get on that boat, my kultanen? You know, the one you tried for in Helsinki."*

As she fingers the amulet she wears around her neck, the tears start again. She says, *"I've been praying that you did. I've been praying that your silence means you're safely on that ship and you just don't have any connectivity. And that soon we will be together again."* Her eyes narrow and darken. *"I will never forgive my parents for not getting you on their ship. They've always been so controlling, but this is evil. I will never —"*

The face of the altar—the screen of the computer—goes blank.

XXXIX

Aprilus 29
Year 242, A.H.

"What's wrong, Lukas?" I clutch his arm. This can't be the end. I have to hear what happened to Elizabet. What really happened, not what I dreamed up for my Chronicle.

"The battery is dead, Eva. I'll have to play with the solar charging."

Battery? Solar charging? He's speaking another language. This is probably how he feels when we Aerie people speak and read in Latin in his presence. "What do you mean?"

"It's hard to explain. I leave for the Boundary lands today. If you'll let me take this back with me, I might be able to recover the rest of Elizabet's story."

"How in the Gods would it help to bring a Relic to the

Boundary lands?" I ask, unable to keep the irritation out of my voice.

Lukas is acting irrationally. He must be playing a card against me. Those who live in the Boundary lands are native to New North—not those chosen by the Gods like the Founders. They are a wild and desperate lot, except for the few selected to serve in the Aerie homes. That's why they need the support and structure of the Aerie rule. They're not all like Lukas.

"Eva, the Boundary lands are nothing like you think. Nor are the Boundary people." Breaking his gaze from the blank altar, he looks up at me. "Tech never died in the Boundary lands, Eva. After the Healing, when all Tech was outlawed, we Boundary people brought it underground and preserved it. I have the tools to fix your computer there."

I am aghast. I stammer. "In-in-in violation of The Lex?"

"Yes. My people are used to keeping secrets. It's part of our history."

"Tech is evil, Lukas. Aren't you afraid of it? Of Apple?"

Lukas takes his hands off the altar and wraps them around mine. "Eva, Tech is not evil in and of itself. Evil depends on the hand that wields it. And Apple is not a god or a demon, no matter what you've been told. The pre-Healing people never thought of Apple as a god. The Apple is just a symbol of their Tech."

I can't bring myself to look at him. I stare down at his hands. If the pre-Healing people never thought of Apple as a god, then my Chronicle is a lie. But how can that be true? I want to believe him, but it goes against everything I've been taught. Against everything that all of New North has been taught. "Is this what you meant that everything I believed in is wrong?"

"In part."

I squeeze my eyes shut. Nothing makes sense right now. Not my appreciation of Elizabet and the pre-Healing life. Not my beliefs about Tech and the supposed false god Apple. Not the Lexors and Basilikons and Archons. Not even The Lex itself.

"If I let you take this . . . thing into the Boundary lands, how will I ever be able to see it again? There's no guarantee that your next assignment will bring us in contact."

"You might just have to come to me."

My eyes fly open. "Seriously?"

"Come on, a Maiden like you who conquered the Taiga, the Tundra, and the Frozen Shores can't handle the Boundary lands?"

I purse my lips. "I'm not in the mood for a joke, Lukas."

There's no humor in his face. "I'm not joking, Eva. There are ways into the Boundary lands that wouldn't require you to scale the Ring or pass through the Gate. And, after all the stories I heard about you from my uncle, I think you can handle the route I have in mind."

"Your uncle?" With each explanation Lukas offers me, I end up more perplexed.

"The Boundary Climber with the streak of white hair. I asked him to look out for you."

So Lukas was with me all along. By proxy, anyway. I find some comfort in the knowledge that not all of my wild imaginings were off-base. I *was* being protected; I just never knew by whom. And it wasn't my father. "That's why he helped me."

Lukas smiles. "So will you come? To the Boundary lands?"

"Even though I could be exiled for trying?" I ask. After the distances I've crossed—to survive beyond the Ring, to

win the Archon Laurels, to endure my grief over Eamon—
does Lukas truly mean for me to jeopardize everything? I
could just as easily say goodbye and forget.

"Don't you think the truth is worth the risk?" he asks.

XL

Maius 20
Year 242, A.H.

bove my bowed head, I hear the Chief Basilikon's words ring throughout the pristine cavernous walls of the Basilika—the most holy place in the Aerie. One cannot enter its massive inner sanctum without sensing that the Gods are there, too. The Sun: through the ice windows far overhead. The Earth: clumped into ancient brown mud that serves as the Chief Basilikon's Highest Altar. The Moon: a sliver through the Moon-holes that line the wall. Now more than ever I feel the Gods' presence. But now, for the first time, I want to shout at them for answers.

"On this morning, we say a special blessing for our new Archon, Eva. Soon, she will embark upon her training, and we ask the Gods for their mercy and counsel as she does. For New North needs a Lex-guided leader."

The Chief Basilkon's voice is like a hot bath. He waves incense over me.

In the rear of the chamber, I hear the Aerie people chant back, "We ask for your blessing, O Gods."

"Archon Eva, you may rise," the Basilkon says.

The Sun's rays, stained blue and red from their passage through the ice windows, warm my cheeks. I know it is Her signal to arise from my genuflection and face the worshippers. As expected from a Maiden and an Archon, I smile in what I hope looks like benevolent thanks for their prayers during this special ceremony just for me. Truly, no matter my misgivings, I am thankful for their wishes. In their faces—my parents, their friends, and all the rest—I see their hopes for the future of New North. And in Jasper's face, I see his aspirations for a future Union. I see truth and stories in all.

But I'm not sure I can give them what they want. I am the lone fraud.

TONIGHT IS THE NIGHT for which I've been waiting twenty-one days. The Moon has shown Herself in full for the first time since Lukas left. I finally have enough light to make my way to the secret opening in the Ring.

It seems that Lukas is right. The truth is worth the risk.

The past twenty-one days have been interminable. I thought that I'd acted at my life before—as a Maiden, a Testor, as a sister past her grief. But I really had no idea what it meant to play a role. Not until the tick I left Lukas on the turret with my Apple Relic and I was forced to pretend to be Eva the Archon, Eva the dutiful daughter, Eva the possible Betrothed. Even though absolutely everything had changed.

The days of so-called freedom before I enter my Archon training have become a prison. I must abide by the rules of my parents' household, the directives of the Aerie society, and the edicts for Maidens before marriage. I must pretend I don't question The Lex, my community, the very history of the Healing, the truth of my people.

During these long days, I learned that I'm not good at the charade. In my *siniks* beyond the Ring, I lost the knack for a double life. So aside from required public engagements, I took exile in this journal and the quiet places of the Aerie. I frequented the diptych in my bedroom and prayer nooks of the Basilika, and everyone acted as though I was purifying myself for the Archon training. It enabled me to avoid Jasper, too. It wasn't simply that I can't face the marriage plans. I've felt a connection I can't even articulate with Jasper since that last *sinik* of the Testing. A Union could represent everything good about life in the Aerie. He's been so supportive since our return, appearing at my side at public events and meals and ceremonies. But I would be unable to hide this change in myself from him for very long.

Even now I feel torn. Yet I know what I must do, even though it means I must leave behind all that I've known and loved. I tell myself I have no choice.

After Evensong bell, I retire to my bedroom, allowing Katja to disrobe me and bundle me into my bedclothes like a baby. The very tick she closes the door behind her, I slide out of bed and into my Testor uniform. I will need its warmth as I cross over into the Boundary lands.

Creaking my bedroom door open as slowly as I dare, I pad down the corridor in my *kamiks*. I've already prepared an excuse should I get caught—I'm mourning Eamon out here on the turret, in our old place—but no one appears as I mount the icy stairs. Reaching into my Testor pack, I pull out an ice screw and carefully twist it into a crevice between the turret tower stones. Once it's secure, I feed the line through the harness I'm wearing under my sealskin cloak and back into the hole. Then I throw the line over the turret wall and belay down.

It's surprisingly easy. As if I was born for this task.

Mapping out the shadows of Her Moonlight across the Aerie, I dart from one darkened corner to the next. Not a soul appears from a home or Keep or town building, not even a Guard. The Aerie is asleep, it seems. Or following The Lex, at least.

In two bells, I reach the base of the Ring. I still need to skirt a very exposed expanse of ice and snow to reach the tiny gap in the Ring that Lukas described. As I wait and watch for the Guards patrolling the rim of the Ring to pass, I realize this is the spot where Eamon fell to his death. I imagine that I can see the smear of blood that for so long stained this section of the Ring, although I know it's been washed away.

I stop. I'm not certain I can press forward. Can I really I pass directly under the place where my brother died? How can I not, after coming so far? As I debate, the shadow of a single Guard appears over the flat white surface of the Ring wall. After his lamplight flickers by, I steel myself and make a run for it.

I count off the ticks necessary to reach the gap—ticks that Lukas painstakingly described—but I don't see the opening. Could I have passed it? I retrace my steps, but I still can't find it. I start to panic, and consider returning home, when I see a black fissure in the Ring's wall of ice. I'd discounted it initially because it resembles nothing more than a spring-time ice crack. But when I squint more closely, it seems wide enough to squeeze through. Lukas had mentioned that the aperture was narrow, but this is dangerously so. Pushing myself along, the gap compresses even farther. It's tight against my chest, and I'm left gasping for air. Any sane person would abandon the attempt as futile. Maybe that's how the Boundary people have protected this pass for so long.

Without warning, the gap opens. There, in a sizable subterranean cave in the base of the Ring, stands Lukas. Broad shoulders and black hair—but stronger and more substantial than he ever seemed in the Aerie. He has waited for me.

XLI

Maius 20
Year 242, A.H.

Without a single word, Lukas takes me by the hand, and we start running. It is pitch black except for Lukas's *naneq* and the jerky light and shadows we cast. I should be scared, but I'm not. Finally, I feel free.

The way is long and twisted; we follow a sinuous and interminable path through the Ring instead of over it. I should tire, but I don't. I feel like I could run forever—until, quite suddenly, the path ends.

This strange tunnel, bored into the Ring at what price I cannot guess, stops mid-air. Lukas and I stand on the edge of a precipice. If it weren't for Lukas's steadying hand, I would have tumbled straight down the face of the cliff. Like my brother.

Down we must climb. I reach for my Testor pack, but gear

isn't necessary. Lukas motions toward the handholds and footholds that have been dug into the frozen wall. Following his lead, I scramble downward and into the Boundary lands.

It looks nothing like I'd been told. Nestled in an outcrop of the Ring, it appears almost cozy. Snug little homes of ice and stone and wood tuck into the Ring wall and into each other, for maximum protection from the biting winds. Little roads connect the numerous structures, and a small town square—not unlike that of the Aerie, except in size—sits at the center.

I realize I never passed the Boundary lands in the Testing, except for the few small huts near the Gate. Those tiny hovels—unkempt, almost tumble-down in appearance—don't resemble this tidy little town at all. They bear the desperate, uncivilized look of the Boundary lands depicted in School-books, created by a people incapable of ruling themselves. A very basic people in need of the Aerie protection and help. I can't help but wonder if maybe those poor huts had been intentionally built near the Gate to foster that exact view. I wonder if anyone lives in them at all.

Lukas makes no effort to hide our approach. His *naneq* swings at his side, casting light in wide arcs. "Aren't you worried someone will see me?" I whisper.

"No, not now that we've made it. Guards never come to this side of the Ring. And no Boundary person would ever tell the Guards or anyone in the Aerie that you're here."

"Even though I'm breaking The Lex?"

"Eva, we don't follow The Lex in the Boundary lands."

I stop walking and stare at him. "You don't?"

He flashes a smile that almost seems pitying. "The Aerie people have to let us live this way, Eva. Free to do as we please. Don't forget—our Hunters and Fishermen supply all the food for the Aerie outside what you grow in the Ark."

Suddenly, I feel defensive of the Aerie. "We help the Boundary lands, too. We give you Ark food and clothes."

"We take your handouts. But we really don't need them. My people have lived on this or land just like it for millennia. We know how to survive without the Ark or the Clothes Keeps, believe me."

"Then why don't you live in the Aerie? With us?"

"Why would we want to? You're not free in there. You live by The Lex, with all those crazy rules." He pauses before we reach the village square and touches my hand for a tick. "I know this is hard for you to understand."

I have so many questions. "If you don't want any part of the Aerie, then why do your people compete for the honor of serving as Boundary Companions and Attendants?"

He laughs. "Is that what they tell you? That we think it's an honor? It's a duty and an obligation that someone from each Boundary family must fulfill. We do it only to keep the peace, not because we want to serve. We might have weapons, but the Aerie people are the only ones with guns. Although I often wonder whether they'd really stand a chance against our *bolas* and spears and bows."

"Guns? Like the Relics Aleksandr and Neils found?"

"Real guns, Eva. Not Relics. The Ring-Guards have working guns." He pauses, as if he's weighing how much more to tell me. How much more I can take. "Eva, we think of the Ring as a prison that locks the Aerie people inside. Not the other way around."

I am stunned into silence. The Boundary lands and people are nothing like I'd been told. Nor is the Aerie. At the same time I know exactly what he means. He used the same word that dominated my thoughts since I saw him last: *prison*.

A few dark-haired, dark-eyed men with *bolas* and blades slung over their shoulders pass us in the opposite direction—obviously out for a hunt. I brace myself for stares or some sort of unusual reaction; it's not every day that and Aerie Maiden walks through the Boundary lands. But they only nod respectfully.

Lukas he raises an eyebrow at me. "Told you." He points to a small thatched roof house. With a plume of smoke rising from a stone chimney, it makes me feel cold. I wonder what it would be like to be inside at its hearth. "That's my house. What do you think?"

"It's nice," I answer honestly.

"You sound surprised."

"It's not exactly as the Teachers described, is it?"

"No," he says, "it wouldn't be."

Lukas pushes open a bright blue door, the color of the crevasse wall. Where did they get the paint to decorate the door so vividly? He calls out: "*Aanak*! We are here."

A shriveled old woman hobbles out of the solar to greet us. Her hair is almost entirely white, and she's wrapped it into a complicated fishtail knot on the top of her head—not unlike the style I wore during the Testing—and fastened it with an elaborately carved whalebone comb. I've never seen someone with such an abundance of wrinkles before; the Aerie people tend not to live long enough to get so many. But when she smiles at me, her whole face lights up, and she is suddenly beautiful. She reminds me of my Nurse Aga. I wonder if Aga is here, too, in this attractive little Boundary town. I'd love to see her again.

"Eva, I am so glad to meet you. I am Lukas's grand-mother, his father's mother," she says.

"Oh." Where are my Maiden manners? I curtsy and say, "It's a pleasure to meet you."

"The pleasure is mine. Your family took good care of Lukas when he served as your brother's Companion, and that means the world to me. You see, I've raised Lukas since he was a little boy when he lost his parents in a hunting accident."

I nod, swallowing. I didn't know that his parents were dead, although I don't think I ever asked about his family before. I guess it's only one of many things I didn't know.

Lukas's *aanak* reaches for my hands and wraps her gnarled fingers around mine. She seems to sense that I'm overwhelmed, and tries to change the course of the conversation. "I have heard many lovely things about you from Lukas. And of course, I am honored to welcome the *Angakkuq* into our family home."

"The *Angakkuq*?"

"Yes, the *Angakkuq*. You know, the shaman." She says, as way of explanation. As if I know.

Yet, the word "shaman" means as little to me as the word *Angakkuq*, and my face must show it. Lukas's *aanak* leans forward and says slowly and clearly, "The *Angakkuq* is the mediator between this world and the spirit world. The seeker of truth. And we've been waiting for a new one for a whole generation."

Lukas's *aanak* must be confused; I've heard that happens to people when they age.

I smile indulgently, and say, "The *Angakkuq*? Oh no, you've mistaken me for someone else. I'm just here to find out more about the pre-Healing person whose Relics I found during the Testing. I'm the new Archon."

She smiles back at me, as if she expected me to demur. "I know you're the new Archon, Eva. I was in the town square. I didn't mistake you for some Maiden climbing the Ring in search of her Boundary Suitor." She laughs at the surprise that must be registering on my face. "You didn't know that occasionally an Aerie Maiden leaves her home for a Boundary future?"

When I shake my head no, she says, "I'm not surprised. Such departures are usually kept quiet in the Aerie. My mother was just such an Aerie Maiden before she left and became the *Angakkuq.*"

So Lukas is part Founder? I reclaim my composure, and say, "Well, I'm just an Archon, not the *Angakkuq.*"

"So it might seem. But often, we don't realize our true *anirniq*—our spirit—until our calling is upon us. Learning the truth about Elizabet Laine and her life as part of your work as Archon is just the first step in uncovering the truth about many other mysteries in your work as *Angakkuq.*"

She smiles enigmatically. What in the Gods is she talking about? I glance over at Lukas, but he shrugs his shoulders. Maybe I'm right. Maybe old age has taken her wits. It's what my parents told me happened to my Nurse Aga when she disappeared one day.

"I will leave you two alone to learn more about Elizabet Laine," she says as she leaves the room.

XLII

Maius 20
Year 242, A.H.

The fire has warmed my body. My muscles sing from the long run, but I am not tired. As if in a dream, I follow Lukas to a corner of the solar where my Apple Relic sits on a table. Bluish light emanates from the Apple symbol, and very thin, seamless skeins of black rope connect the Relic to another silver box.

What are those for? They don't look like the sealskin ropes to which I'm accustomed. "I've been able to get it to work," he explains.

"Thank the Gods," I say. "I'm glad you didn't hurt it."

Lukas glances over at me with an odd expression, but remains silent. He then pulls over the solar's two chairs to the table, and we sit before the glowing surface. He taps a few of the squares on one side of it, and the face comes alive again. "I found one more post from Elizabet, and a bunch of books that she kept on the computer. I thought you'd like to see everything."

I nod. My throat feels very dry. "Do we have time?"

"I think we can cram in the most important stuff before you have to go back."

My heart leaps at the sight of Elizabet, almost as if she's a friend just back from a trip beyond the Ring. A friend in desperate need of help. She looks more haggard than when I saw her last, even though she's in the same clothes and in the same room.

Tears pour down her face, and she makes no attempt to wipe them off. She makes no effort to look pretty anymore.

"Robert, where are you? It's been two days since your last post, and I've heard nothing from you, my kultanen. Nothing."

She clasps a small, leather-bound book between her hands and strokes it like some kind of talisman. The book has a lower-case letter "t" on the front. I hold my breath, waiting for her to tell me her secrets again. She draws very close to the computer face and reaches out to touch it. As if she's stroking a Betrothed's face. *"I keep praying. I keep studying the Bible, and looking for some kind of sign that you're still out there. Alive. When so many others are dead. Are you, my kultanen? Are you still alive?"*

There's a crash. The entire room in which Elizabet stands tilts to the left. All the objects on tables fly to the floor. Water starts pouring down the walls. And Elizabet is nowhere to be found, but I hear her screams.

I find myself screaming, too.

In a few ticks, Elizabet's face reappears. Blood streams from her forehead and she's breathing heavily, but her gaze is steady. The wound is not fatal.

"I'm okay. The captain told me this might happen. The ship's GPS gave out yesterday, and we are sailing blind in waters littered with icebergs. I'm pretty sure we just hit one. What else could put a huge hole in a ship this size?" She laughs crazily and wipes the blood out of her eyes. *"I don't know if I'll have the connectivity to make another post again, Robert. But if you're still out there, my kultanen, please know that I love you."* She places her fingers on her lips, kisses them, and reaches them toward the computer screen. *"And if you can, when all this madness is over, look for me on that Arctic island I told you about. If I make it there, that is. They call it New North."*

The computer face grows fuzzy. Elizabet fastens the amulet around her neck, straps her pink pack on her back, and closes the computer. Then the screen goes black.

XLIII

Maius 20
Year 242, A.H.

I am sobbing. Lukas reaches out and touches my arm. "I know it's hard to watch, Eva. But remember, this happened almost two hundred and fifty years ago. Elizabet's *anirniq* has long been at peace. You saw her bones."

He clenches my hand tightly as we stare at the black computer screen together. My face is wet with tears, just like hers. I'm not certain whether I'm crying over the loss of Elizabet's life or my own, the life I'd always known.

"Elizabet died right after that post," I say. It isn't a question. I know it for a fact.

"Yes."

"The ship never made it to New North."

"No. Not with her alive, anyway."

"You didn't find any other posts?"

"Nope. Just this one and the other one that you saw. I wish we had her flash drive."

"Flash drive?"

"It's a file that stores things like her posts. She wore it around her neck. You saw it on in that last image. In the other post, she mentioned that she placed Robert's last video on it."

"Do you mean the amulet?" I ask, even though the word sounds wrong. I pull Elizabet's necklace out from beneath my sealskin cloak.

Lukas's eyes grow wide. "You've had it this whole time?"

"I didn't realize what it was. I thought she used it to offer up prayers to Apple."

"Even though I told you they didn't pray to Apple? That Apple was just some stupid symbol of the Tech?" Lukas sounds angry.

How dare he get mad at me? After all he's asked of me. "Why are you talking to me like that? I'm telling you what I believed at the time. What was right to believe."

Lukas casts a quick glance toward the shadowy hall here his *aanak* disappeared. Perhaps he's worried she'll hear us. But his eyes soften and he nods. Not deferentially—he hasn't treated me with deference at all since he took my hand and we started running. Like an equal. "I'm sorry, Eva. You're right."

He gently takes this mysterious thing and sticks the silver head into the side of the . . . computer. I can no longer think of it as an altar. I know that now if I am to see its truth, even though the word "computer" has no meaning.

Just like I thought: it is a sort of a puzzle piece—only I'd never have guessed exactly what kind of puzzle. The screen brightens and comes alive again.

This time, though, we're not gazing at Elizabet. A handsome young man—definitely a Gallant if he'd lived in the Aerie—appears. His dark hair and fair, freckled cheeks are wet, and his bright green eyes look kind of wild. He stands on a windy, crowded dock.

It must be Robert.

"Elizabet, my kultanen. I'm thinking of you snug and safe on your parents' icebreaker ship. Heading toward some polar island where your family's set up camp—as only they could manage at the world's end. You've always rejected their money and their grand designs for you and your life. Even for the sake of your trashy English boyfriend. Now I'm damned grateful for them. For the chance they're giving you.

"It's madness here at the docks, but I'm determined to get on one of these ships leaving the Helsinki harbor. My brother Alex has a friend from University who's training as a marine biologist on one of the scientific boats. He's trying to gain us passage. The ship's called the Kalevala. *I hope the name is a good omen."*

He looks away from the computer, toward the crowds. And then he speaks to the computer again, his voice low and quick. *"Remember your debut as Juliet at the Mariinsky? You looked so exquisite on the stage, so effortless in your pirouettes and leaps. I felt I was the only one who knew how long you worked. How much you practiced to make everything appear so fluid and easy. How much you sacrificed to pursue your dream. Leaving Finland. Leaving me.*

"Well, we are still together, my kultanen, are we not? Even now. Even as the polar ice caps melt and flood our world. What's that famous line from Shakespeare's Romeo and Juliet? *From the last ballet I saw you perform? 'Good night, good night. Parting is such sweet sorrow, that I shall say good night till it be morrow.'"* His voice catches. *"We aren't really parting, are we, my*

kultanen? Just saying good night until the morrow. That is what I shall whisper on board the Kalevala, *as we get closer and closer to you and this place, New North. Too good to be true, I think. An oasis, like from a myth. But I'll try to believe. I have to. Until then, my kultanen, good night, good night, good night."*

He touches the screen and it darkens. "I don't think I could stand another tick," I admit. "Thank the Gods that screen is black." I feel heartbroken and numb and angry and guilty all at once. Guilty because I'm glad it's over. And heartbroken because I feel more bound to Elizabet than ever. Robert offered her what Lukas offered me: the promise that he would believe. For different reasons, obviously, but the word is aflame again. *Believe.*

Even Lukas seems moved. "It's too hard, knowing what we know about them."

I shake my head, doubt gnawing away at my thoughts. "Elizabet isn't really the same person I wrote about in the Chronicle, is she? She loved to dance, and she made huge sacrifices to do it. She wasn't forced. Dancing wasn't the tawdry spectacle that we were taught about in School."

I look at Lukas. He lowers his eyes.

"No, she's not the Elizabet from the Chronicle," he concedes.

"She seems ambitious—even a little ruthless. I mean, she abandoned her boyfriend and her family—defied her family's wishes, even. For her own dream." I pause; the words are hard to form and to speak. "It makes me wonder whether I understand any part of the pre-Healing history at all."

Privately, I laud her strength. I wonder if it was common in pre-Healing women. Maybe they were tough and didn't need the protection of Gallants.

"The Golden Age," Lukas says quietly.

I frown at him. What do you mean?"

"The period of history, the one that the Aerie rulers say they used as inspiration for their own—"

"I know what the Golden Age is," I whisper, cutting him off.

Lukas starts tapping away at those rectangular keys. "Take a look at this. Elizabet's computer stored a bunch of books." He points to the screen. "One of them is called *Life in a Medieval Village in the Golden Age.*"

I squint at a gorgeously vibrant painting, filled with images that are not unlike the Aerie: stone walls of a distant Keep, men and women in plain robes. The huts that dominate the foreground seem more like Lukas's village, however.

"I think it's a Schoolbook of some sort," he continues. "Maybe Elizabet was still doing some studies. She looks young enough to still be in School."

"She was eighteen." I say quietly. "Exactly my age."

Lukas clicks and words appear. Shoulders touching, we draw close. He touches the screen, whirling me to particular passages. The language is dense and dry, but I get it in a tick, a heartbeat. Talk of hunger, of servitude, of ignorance. Everything of value concentrated in the hands of a few. This was no Golden Age. So why does The Lex paint it that way? New North *is* better than this. Everyone—Boundary and Aerie—has adequate food, clothing, and shelter. It almost seems as if the Founders of New North built a society that's like my Chronicle of Elizabet. On the outside, it could appear to be true. But there is no real truth.

After about a bell, my head is spinning. "Lukas." My voice shakes. "I don't know what is real anymore."

"That's how Eamon felt, too," he answers, keeping his eyes fixed to words on the glowing screen.

I grab his shoulder. "Eamon knew about all this?"

"Yes, he'd learned something of the gap between now and the real past. But, Eva," Lukas breaks his gaze from the computer and clasps his hand on mine. "I don't want you to end up like Eamon."

XLIV

Maius 20
Year 242, A.H.

Panic takes hold. I crane my neck, looking for his grand-mother. Where is she? As odd and confusing as she is, I want her here; I want to be rescued from the news I sense Lukas is about to give me. Maybe she got out of the way for this very reason.

I try to wriggle out of his grasp. "What do you mean 'end up like Eamon'? Seeing this stuff doesn't mean I'll go careening down the side of the Ring. One has nothing to do with the other."

He is insistent that we hold hands; he takes the other. "Eva, they have everything to do with one another. Eamon knew that The Lex was a fiction. That everything you were raised to believe was a fiction."

I gasp at the word. "A fiction?"

Lukas's voice is firm. "Yes. Eamon discovered something very dangerous. He learned that the story of the Healing was the same as an old, banned story about a flood that wiped clean the past. That story was in a book called the Bible. And people like Robert and Elizabet believed in the Bible as you believe in The Lex."

Bible. Haven't I just heard that word?

Lukas continues. "The Bible was kind of like a pre-Healing Lex. For some people, at least. Elizabet was holding a copy of the Bible in her hands during her last post. She mentioned praying with it, when she was hoping for a post from Robert."

"Is the Bible about Apple? Do you have a copy?" The questions tumble out of my mouth. Even in my bewilderment, it's as if my appetite for truth has just been whet, and I am starving for answers.

He seems annoyed, or maybe just tired. He sighs. "No, we don't have a copy. And it's not about Apple. Tech came long after the Bible. Anyway, all Bibles were destroyed. We out here in the Boundary lands have never forgotten it, though."

"How do you know that?"

"We pass down the past word by word, Eva. So my people have kept our own record of what happened here in New North before and after the Healing. And we remember when the Bibles were destroyed."

"Why would the Founders have destroyed those books? Paper is precious."

He lets go of my hands. He no longer sounds tired; he sounds angry. "Because the Founders needed to write a fiction. So they took the parts of the Bible that worked and fashioned The Lex out of them."

I'm angry, too. "That's heresy, Lukas. The Lex is a sacred

work, delivered directly to the people of New North by the Gods."

"And everything that you've been taught has turned out to be true, right?" he snaps back.

I don't answer. How can I? This one trip to the Boundary lands has burned every single one of my long-held beliefs. About the Aerie, the pre-Healing days, the Healing itself, The Lex . . . and now my own twin.

Lukas speaks to my silence. "Please look at this, Eva." He taps on the computer again and pulls up another book that Elizabet stored on it. "I might not have a copy of the Bible, but Elizabet did. Here it is, on her computer."

I push him to the side. Neither one of us wants him to spoon-feed me information anymore. I want to make my own decisions about Elizabet, the Healing, New North, and Eamon. No longer do I want to view the present or the past through anyone else's prism. Imitating Lukas's motions, I page through this . . . *Bible*. The words and rhythm remind me of The Lex. The language that is at once beautiful and obtuse.

His hand jerks out to stop me at a passage.

I read the words over and over to myself, until I realize that I need to speak them aloud. "*In the eyes of God, the Earth was corrupt and full of lawlessness. When God saw how corrupt man had become, God said, "I will wipe out from the Earth mankind whom I have created, and not only mankind, but also the beasts and the creeping things and the birds of the air." Then God said to Noah, 'Make yourself an ark . . . Go into the ark, you and all your household, for you and you alone in this age have I found to be truly just and chosen . . . I will bring rain down on the Earth for forty days and forty nights, and so I will wipe out from the surface of the earth every moving creature that I have made . . .'*"

I grow quiet. Lukas doesn't say anything, and he doesn't need to. We both know just how much "The Story of Noah"—a tale from pre-Healing times, from pre Golden-Age times—reads like the creation story in The Lex, supposedly divined to the Founders only two hundred and fifty years ago.

As if to comfort me, Lukas offers, "My people—who were once called the Inuit—have a flood myth, too. Perhaps all people do."

"Do you mean the story of the Mariner?" Nurse Aga had told me the tale of the Mariner, who survived a great flood that covered the Earth but for a tall, icy mountain by making a raft. But I never connected that story with our history in The Lex.

"Where did you hear that?" Lukas looks alarmed.

"From my Nurse Aga. Before she became so old—so dotty, my parents called it—that she had to come back to the Boundary lands."

"That's what your parents told you about this woman?"

"Yes." I don't like how Lukas refers to Nurse Aga. I'm afraid to find out more; I don't think I can handle it right now if something awful happened to her. So instead, I ask, "How do you know all this, Lukas? You sound like a Teacher."

"We all would to you. Our memories are long. We remember well the times before the Healing."

"But how did Eamon learn about it? Did you tell him?"

"No, I didn't tell him. Do you remember when he spent all that time in the Archives, studying past Testing?"

"Of course. We fought about that."

"He had come across a journal from a past Testor. The journal was over one hundred and fifty years old, and it contained references to the Bible and the Noah story. It seems that our people aren't the only ones who remembered."

"And he told *you* about what he found?" The manner of Eamon's epiphany is coming clearer. But why did he tell Lukas instead of me? To protect me? Or because he didn't trust me, as I was just a Maiden and unequipped to handle the truth?

Lukas studies my face as realization after realization dawns. "And I shared with him what I knew. What my people know."

Confusion melts away, like ice floes in the sun. I know now why he was so scared, so intent on his training. But one huge block remains. "I still don't get what this has to do with Eamon's death."

"Eva, Eamon wanted to win the Archon spot to uncover the full truth about New North. But someone found out about Eamon's knowledge and his intentions. So, before he could become the Archon and change everything, he was killed."

I shake my head. This is impossible. Eamon was alone out there. "Who?"

"We don't know. Our best guess is someone in the Aerie did it, someone with a lot to lose if Eamon became the Archon. But that could be so many different people. Or one of many different factions."

"Like?"

"Well, the Triad—or one of their minions—is an obvious choice. But they could have been oblivious to Eamon's work, and it could easily be one of their lesser cogs who had a lot at stake if Eamon really changed the rules of the Aerie. Or it could be one of the other Testors."

Faces and names flash through my mind. The Triad? There is no way my father could have been involved in such an act, no matter the consequences. Unless some rogue member had the foresight to set me up to be the Archon because he believed I'd be a malleable Maiden? What about the Testors? Aleksandr, Neils, the others? Murder seems beyond their small selves, but it's possible. Jasper? No, that's ridiculous.

What about someone like Scout Okpik, who looked Boundary-born but benefitted so much from the Aerie ways? It would certainly explain his behavior toward me. He needed to make sure that I didn't stand a chance of winning, just in case I knew what Eamon knew, and he became uninterested in me once he believed I no longer had a shot.

I feel sick. I start to retch and run out the front door. Lukas races out after me and holds back my hair as I empty the meager contents of my stomach in a snow bank just outside.

Once my breathing has evened, Lukas leads me back inside. He settles me onto a chair and moves to the kitchen. When he returns, he has a cup of steaming tea with him. I'm guessing his *aanak* prepared it for me. Has she been listening to our conversation? I bet she knows everything that Lukas has told me. Even before he said it aloud.

As he sits down in the other chair, Lukas opens his mouth. Then he closes it and takes a moment. "We of the Boundary have always suspected the same things that Eamon learned, but we've never known the full truth about the Healing and the state of our Earth. Only someone on the inside—someone with access to the information that the Triad has hidden away—could do that. Eamon wanted to be that person. I'm not talking about Chief Archon. I'm talking about someone who could bridge the many worlds with the truth."

Now I see where he's going. Why he brought me out here. It wasn't simply to show me the secrets of Elizabet Laine. "He would have become the *Angakkuq*. He was the one your people have been waiting for. Like your *aanak* wants?" I ask.

"I guess so, Eva," he says.

I whisper, mostly to myself. "So this is what Eamon meant. *'Will they still love me when I do what I must?'*"

Lukas stares hard at me over the steaming tea. "What did you say to him when he asked that question?"

For some reason, I don't want to tell Lukas about the journal entries. Instead, I create a fiction. Why shouldn't I? "Just that I would love him no matter what. But I am the Archon now. I will find out the truth—just like Eamon would have done."

"No, Eva. I don't think you should. It's too dangerous, and they'd be watching you. After what happened with Eamon."

I'm surprised. I was expecting Lukas to summon his *aanak*. To tell me what I could do in Eamon's place.

Lukas's voice grows urgent. "Why not stay here, disappear into the Boundary lands with me? We have ways of hiding people. If you really feel you have to continue Eamon's legacy, why not undertake it more safely, from this side of the Ring? With me helping you?"

I draw back. "Why would you have encouraged me to come to the Boundary lands and hear Elizabet's story unless you wanted me to learn the truth? Unless you wanted me to become the *Angakkuq*? "

Lukas shakes his head. "Maybe part of me wanted that, Eva. At the start. But now that you're here, and now that I stare into your eyes, I don't want you to become an Archon or the *Angakkuq*." He lunges for me and grabs my shoulders, so forcefully that it hurts. "Do you really want to end up like your brother? Please don't do this to me."

"It has nothing to do with you, Lukas."

"Are you blind? Can't you see how I feel about you?"

I stare into his dark eyes, and see more truths. Maybe they were always there. Maybe I overlooked underneath Lukas's stoicism. Maybe I've suppressed them in myself too. The Maiden in me—so trained in the ways of modesty—tries to convince me to lower my gaze and play dumb. But I fight her, and answer honestly, "I think I do, Lukas."

"Do you share my feelings at all? I know it's forbidden by your precious Lex, but even just a hint of—"

I press my finger to his lips. I think I do share his feelings—at least, a little—but we can't think about them. Besides, I need time with my feelings. And I don't have time. So I say, "How can I possibly act on that now?"

He kisses my finger and lets it go. "So where does that leave us?"

I say the answer he already knows. "I must fulfill Eamon's destiny."

XXXXV

Maius 20
Year 242, A.H.

I allow myself a single, final indulgence. As Lukas and I hurry back through the Boundary lands and into the centuries-old tunnel through the Ring, I hold his hand. And I permit myself to fantasize about a life I will never have. An honest life with Lukas.

Before I squeeze through the narrow part of the passage, Lukas and I pause for an awkward moment to say our farewells. Will I ever see him again? He will be re-assigned to the Aerie, and there our paths might cross as Maiden and Attendant or Archon and Attendant, depending on when and where we meet. But it will never be the same as this moment. We will never have this freedom again, alone with our truths.

Lukas answers my unspoken question. "I'll never really

leave you, Eva. Even when you don't see me, I'll be watching over you."

"Just like you did during the Testing?"

He smiles. "Much the same way. I'll find a way to keep tabs on what you're doing. My people are everywhere and nowhere. You know that now. And I'll find a way to protect you—even get you out of the Aerie if need be—if you really insist on moving forward with Eamon's mission."

"I'd like that, Lukas. It would make me feel less alone."

"You'll never be alone, Eva. I promise you."

I don't want this moment to end, but I'm starting to get scared. Daylight is coming soon, and with it, the distinct possibility of discovery. I must make my way back to the Aerie and into my warm, downy bed before I'm found out. Or I'll never get to start my work as the *Angakkuq*, as Archon, as Eamon's successor. I release his hand. "Take good care of Elizabet's Relic, Lukas."

"I will, Eva. Remember what I told you about where to look for information. Look for Tech and the old stories; the truth will lie there. Remember what I taught you about not getting caught. And . . . believe."

"I will. Goodbye, Lukas."

He grabs my hand one last time. "What was it Robert said to Elizabet? 'I shall say good night till it be morrow.' Good night, Eva."

I break away from him before I start crying.

WHEN THE ICE WALLS narrow and squeeze down tightly on my chest, I welcome the sensation. It forces me to think about something other than the revelations of this night. I finally push through the gap and out into the crisp night air, gasping for breath. And happy about the distraction. When I look up—and around—I freeze. I'm not alone.

Jasper is waiting for me on the other side of the Ring.

"What in the Gods are you doing out here?" I nearly shout, then bite my lip.

"I could ask you the very same question. It's not safe for you to be out here," he says. His voice is oddly toneless.

"Nor for you. Did you follow me?"

"Yes."

My eyes narrow. "How far?"

"Only to this spot."

"Why would you take such a risk?"

"I've been concerned about you."

"So you thought you'd hide outside my family's home and follow me in the dead of the night?" I figure that, if I act offended, he might not pry so hard into my whereabouts. "What have I ever done to make you trust me so little?"

He bows his head. "You've been so cold, so removed, ever since we got back from the Testing. You only talk to me—or smile at me—when we're in some public place. Anyone would think I'd won the Archon Laurels and you were mad at me."

"You know better than that, Jasper. Why didn't you visit me at home? Instead of stalking me?"

He lifts his head, his eyes flashing in the light of Her Moon. "Do you think I haven't tried to see you at home? You're always at the Basilika, or off in your room praying to the Gods at the diptych."

I offer him up the only plausible excuse and silently beg my poor brother for forgiveness for invoking his name this way. I fight to keep the desperation out of my voice. "Jasper, since I've gotten back from the Testing, I've been struggling with my grief over Eamon. Before we left, I had the Testing to focus on. But now, I feel the loss of Eamon everywhere."

His eyes are glistening now. "Eva, I'm sorry. And here I've been selfishly thinking it had something to do with me. How stupid of me."

It's his Gallant voice, yet I know it's sincere. And I actually feel terrible that he believes my fiction so readily. But since it's working, I take it one step further. "That's why I'm out here tonight."

"What do you mean?"

"This is the spot where my brother died. I woke up in the middle of the night, and I felt compelled to come out here and say goodbye to him. I thought it would help me put him to rest."

Jasper reaches out for my hand. I take it. "I understand, Eva."

A bright blueish light flashes down on from above. It's a Ring-Guard on his rounds. How could I have been so stupid as to stand here and chat with Jasper? Not for a tick should I have forgotten that the real threat comes from above.

Instinctively, we duck down, as if that would hide us at all. Hands linked, we start to run toward the town. Even though we're horribly exposed.

"Halt!"

We keep running. I hear the Warning Bell sound in the distance—jarring and dissonant—unlike the daily bells that govern the Aerie life. Two Ring-Guards run toward us, brandishing lamps that produce the same unholy Tech glow. It occurs to me that I've never witnessed what happens during an actual Warning Bell. And I recognize the black tubular devices. They look just like the one I found in Elizabet's pink pack. My jaw tightens. The Aerie leaders use Tech for their own purposes. My father among them. He will answer me soon enough. This is what Lukas meant by needing someone on the inside to discern the truth.

I have only one chance to rescue myself—and Jasper—from this mess. I slow my pace. I square my shoulders. And I stare at the Ring-Guards. Both are thick and strong; they could crack me in half like a fire log. The heavier one scurries forward.

"What in the Gods do you think you are doing?" I ask, imperiously.

"How dare you speak to us that way!" he barks.

I do not flinch. Instead, I answer, "How dare *you*? Don't you recognize your new Archon?"

The Ring-Guard lowers his arm, slowly. He's still suspicious, but I watch as they take in my Testor uniform. And my face.

The smaller Ring-Guard cries, "By the Gods, you're Eva!"

"Yes. If either one of you stood in the town square twenty-one days ago when the Testing ended, you would have seen me wearing the Archon Laurels."

The first Ring-Guard looks me up and down. Frost coats his beard. His eyes flash to Jasper. "That doesn't give you the right to be out at the Ring in the dead of night."

My heart is pounding, but I pray to the Gods that he can't hear my voice quiver. Attitude is everything right now. That, and my knowledge of The Lex.

"In truth it does. The Lex explicitly states that Archons—along with Lexors and Basilkons—have the right to travel at will, regardless of the hour."

The Ring-Guards are silent. I know that this is beyond their limited knowledge of right and wrong. The smaller says, "She's right. Let's just walk away. Imagine the squawking if we tried to arrest New North's Archon heroine."

The first Ring-Guard backs away, then stops. "I'm willing to let her go. But what about him?" He points to Jasper. "He's no Archon. I saw him stand on the stage next to her. He lost the Testing."

I will myself to stand taller. "Do not insult this Gallant."

"That's no insult, just simple truth. He's got to obey The Lex like the rest of us."

I smile at him. "Really? He has the right to be out here, same as me."

"Oh yeah? Why is that, Maiden Archon?"

There's only one thing I can say that will save Jasper right now. Words that The Lex tells us cannot be unsaid once said. Can I really seal my fate to rescue Jasper from the gallows? Will I be able to fulfill my destiny if I do? I have no other choice. I swallow hard.

"Because he is my Betrothed."

The Praebulum

We, the Founders of New North, join together in memorializing this Praebulum. The Gods themselves have divined the words we write, so in truth, the words are Gods-made and not of man. The Gods know that, as we come together to birth this society of New North, we need Their guidance and Their blessings. The words of this Praebulum and the accompanying Lex are Their mandates for us—the Gods' chosen people—and our charges—the people of the Boundary. We must faithfully abide by Their dictates to ensure that the Gods need never again visit the Healing upon us.

The Healing was necessary, this we know. Mankind was worshipping the false god Apple. With its modern siren's song, that demon Apple had lured mankind into venerating his evil minions—Tech and meds and currency and corruption of ourselves and world.

Mankind had forgotten to honor the true Gods—our Mother Sun and our Father Earth, among them—and to live according to Their simple, yet powerful, ways. Mankind had become corrupt in Their eyes.

The Gods could tolerate it no longer. The Gods swept hurricanes across the world and warmed the polar ice caps—washing the Healing over mankind. For their sins, Father Earth was determined to eradicate all evidence of human life and rose His seas over nearly all His lands. At the last possible tick, He listened to Mother Sun's pleas for mercy; He permitted Her rays to sink behind the clouds and lower the temperature of the seas, thereby sparing one last piece of land. He allowed Her to lead us—the sole righteous people on His earth, the chosen ones—to a fleet of boats, the Arks. Then He permitted Her to deliver us to the surviving land of New North.

Yet, the Gods' mercy has its limits. We must ardently follow the Gods' rules for our new world as embodied in this Praebulum and The Lex—or risk the Healing again. In so doing, we must reject the false brightness of Apple's modern Neon age and ferret out any and all remaining evidence of its artificial luminescence. We must fashion a society that lives in the natural world as the Gods made it before the wickedness of Apple's modernity took hold. The Gods call us to live as people did in that earlier, more innocent and idyllic time—the Golden Age of the Medieval era.

We must do everything just as the Gods command us in The Lex. We must create the perfect society in the Gods' eyes. There will be no second chances.

The Gods have revealed to us the perfect structure of our new society in New North. Herein, we set forth the specific roles that the Gods command each of us to fill. In this way, every man and woman in New North—be they Aerie or Boundary—will know their place and their duties, and their will be no cause for transgression. We will leave to The Lex the remaining details of the idyllic Golden Age society the Gods order us to create.

The Triad: The Gods' Leaders in New North

The Gods mandate that The Lex will guide every facet of mankind's existence, yet They acknowledge that They must have representatives in New North to propagate and enforce The Lex. Thus, They have ordered that we create the Triad, who will balance equally the power bestowed upon them by the Gods.

The Triad's authority derives from the Gods' power, and thus, the three arms of the Triad must be seen as the Gods' own. The first arm of the Triad is that of the Lexors. The Lexors will serve as the hammer of the Gods; they will be the tool instrumental in binding us together, loud and forceful when they must strike. Each year, the strongest and most steadfast eighteen-year-old in the Aerie will be picked for the role of Lexor in the Forge competition. The Lexors will be specially trained in The Lex and its interpretation, and will assist the Basilikons and Archons in their duties. A Chief Lexor will be selected to serve over the Lexors based on his past performance in the Forge, and he will serve a ten-year term, at which time he will relinquish his title to the next Chief and return to the role of Lexor.

The second arm of the Triad is that of the Basilikons. The Basilikons will serve as our sacred orb, the constant, living reminder of our celestial Gods, our Mother Sun and our Father Earth, among them. Each year, through the competition of the Fasting, the most faithful and pious eighteen-year-old in the Aerie will be selected to assist in presiding over the Gods' rituals in the Basilika. A Chief Basilikon will be selected to serve over the Basilikons based on his past performance in the Fasting, and he will serve a ten-year term, at which time he will relinquish his title to the next Chief and return to the role of Basilikon.

The third arm of the Triad is that of the Archons. The Archons will serve as our chisel, the instrument necessary in unearthing the memories of our flawed past and the living reminder of our commitment to the Golden Age path. The most tenacious and insightful eighteen-year-old in Aerie shall compete for the honor in the Testing. A Chief Archon will be selected to serve over the Archons based on his past perfor-mance in the Testing, and he will serve a ten-year term, at which time he will relinquish his title to the next Chief and return to the role of Archon.

The hammer, the orb, and the chisel. To become part of the Triad is to become the living embodiment of the Gods in New North. These roles are sacred, as are the competitions that yield its members. They must be: The Triad and The Lex are all that stand between the people of New North and another Healing.

The Aerie People: The Chosen Ones

We of the Aerie are the Gods' chosen people. When the Earth permitted the Sun to spare us—and spare one last piece of land for us to inhabit—He did so because we were righteous in our faith in Them. We must continue to deserve this bless-ing—and our status as Founders of this land—by fulfilling the important roles selected for us by Them. Even though we might not all attain the status of Triad, every role is critical for the ongoing survival of New North and must be considered a hallowed task.

Every member of a Founding Family—and his or her descendants—will live in the protected enclave of the Aerie and fulfill one of the following places in our society. While only Keepers may be called Lord and Lady, every adult man in the Aerie shall be considered a Gentleman, every adult woman a Gentlewoman, every youthful male a Gallant, and every youthful female a Maiden—no matter the height of his or her calling. Although each Aerie man and woman, boy and girl, will bear these titles and serve in these roles, they will also be given their our individual name, known as their Water-name.

> The Keepers—Each resource necessary for life in New North will be maintained as a Keep, and the head of each Founding Family will serve as the resource's Keeper. For example, all non-indigenous food will be grown in the converted Ark, and a Founding Family member will be Keeper of the Ark.

> The Stewards—Each Keeper will have a team of Stewards to assist him or her in the running of his or her Keep. The Stewards must come from Founding Families, and the Keepers will assign the Stewards appropriate responsibilities within the Keep.

> The Guards—The tenuous peace of our new land must be kept by the Guards, from within and without. The men for this dangerous role will be picked from the ranks of the Founding Families.

While the Triad, Keepers, Stewards, and Guards will ensure that New North provides its peoples with all the necessities for life—and that the Gods' rules are followed—the Ladies, Gentlewomen, and Maidens of the Aerie will also have a special, sacred role. They will be responsible for keeping the hearth and home. They will ensure the adherence to the Gods' rules within that domain. The manner in which they do so—as well as the ways in which their Marital Union will be selected and their children borne, for those too are consecrated duties and our race too precious to leave to chance—will be detailed in The Lex.

The Boundary People: Our Charges

When the Gods delivered us to the shores of New North, we discovered that we were not alone. The Arctic island that became New North was inhabited by a group of indigenous folk who lived here long before the Healing. This population we now call the Boundary people, because they live in a protected area around the boundary of the Aerie. The best among them will be selected to serve in the Aerie homes as Attendants, Companions, and Nurses; otherwise, they will perform Lex-ordered functions in their own Boundary land.

These people are not chosen by the Gods, like ourselves. Instead, the Gods bestowed these disadvantaged peoples upon us as charges, for whom we must provide safekeeping and care. Much as the Gods provide us with safekeeping and care. If we fail in this sanctified test, then we fail in the second chance the Gods have given us. We must succeed.

The Gods delivered this Praebulum to us so that we might comprehend the importance of our places in New North, and abide by our roles and Their laws. The story of our New North's Founding and the details of Their laws may be found in the accompanying Lex. This shall serve as the guide for all of mankind . . . so that the Healing will never happen again.

Year 8, A.H.

About the author

HEATHER TERRELL worked as a commercial litigator in New York City for over ten years, but she has always been obsessed with myth, lore, and the gap between history and the truth. This preoccupation has led to several loosely factual historical novels (*The Chrysalis, The Map Thief, Brigid of Kildare*) and the pure-lore *Fallen Angel* series. *Relic* is the first installment of The Books of Eva series. She lives in Pittsburgh with her family. Visit her at www.heatherterrell.com.

About the illustrator

RICARDO CORTÉS has written and illustrated books about everything from Coca-Cola to Chinese food to the Jamaican bobsled team. He also illustrated the #1 *New York Times* best-selling international sensation *Go the F**k to Sleep*. But it all started with his research laboratory, the Magic Propaganda Mill. Visit him at: www.rmcortes.com